Digging Deep

The cross he bears is not the burden he carries.

Sam Ransom

Digging Deep
By Sam Ransom

ISBN: 979-8-9856367-0-3 - Paperback
ISBN: 979-8-9856367-1-0 - Hardcover
ISBN: 979-8-9856367-2-7 - Ebook

FIRST EDITION

First Printing 2023

Printed in the United States of America
Library of Congress Cataloging in Publication Data on file.

Published by

MANIFESTED PUBLISHING

DEDICATION

To the best part of me:
Sécha, I love you and the journey we share.

To the brightest light to enter the world since Jesus:
Aniyah and Trinity, "I love you 'more'!"

1

"Consider the lilies of the field, how they grow: they neither toil nor spin; and yet I say to you that even Solomon in all his glory was not arrayed like one of these."

Matthew 6:28-29

If there is such a thing as the perfect day, then May 18, 2005, was it. The rolling, grassy fields were festooned with thousands of blooming daisies, creating a maize sea that rivaled the sun. The beautiful Gloria Trudeau was smiling from ear to ear, watching the man of her dreams devolve into the young boy that her little girls loved to play with. Solomon Trudeau was the merry-go-round—his two little girls holding onto his arms as he spun and spun and spun. Their dainty little feet flew through the air. Their precious laughter warmed the hearts of everyone within earshot.

"Again, Daddy!" Bethany pleaded. "Spin us again!" Bethany was four years old, Solomon's oldest daughter. Her energy knew no bounds. She could play until pigs fly, and then some! Solomon, ever the proud, doting dad, happily obliged, though he had to change direction so he didn't lose his breakfast along with his balance. "Best day everrrrrrr!" screamed Simone, holding tightly as the world flew past her round and round. Simone was his youngest, only three years old. It *was* the best day ever!

What made that day so special wasn't just the joy in Solomon's heart or the laughter from his little girls, or the soft kisses and warm embrace from Gloria. That day was the end of innocence. It was a day they enjoyed like it was their last—because they thought it very well could be.

In two days, Solomon would pack his rucksack and get on a C-5 headed for Iraq. President Bush—the second one—had opened up a can of whoop-ass on Saddam Hussein, and now it was Solomon's turn to defend freedom in the middle of the desert.

Behind Gloria's smile lurked a hurting heart. Her first and only true love was leaving her for the first time—and quite possibly the last. They had known each other since middle school. He started proposing during their junior year, but she didn't say yes. Matter of fact, she *never* said yes! It wasn't that she didn't love him. On the contrary, she was madly in love with him, ever since the day he beat up Charlie Simpson for pushing her out of the lunch line because he was too hungry to wait. (Everyone knew Gloria Cooper took forever to decide what she wanted for lunch.) No, she definitely wanted to marry him, but she already had a ring on *that* finger.

On her fifteenth birthday, Gloria's daddy put on his best suit and took her to a real fancy restaurant. He got down on one knee and "proposed" to her. He said, "Glo-worm"—that was his nickname for her—"will you be my girl until *we* find the man that God has prepared for you?" He slipped a beautiful diamond ring (. 25 carat is huge to a sophomore!) on her finger and kissed her on the forehead. From that day forward, he taught her that "any man who really loves you will wait for you and only you." He also told her that "before you have kids, you have to get married, and before you get married, you have to graduate from college." So the evening she graduated from college, she drove 135 miles to surprise Solomon, who was finishing up exams. She dropped down on one knee and asked him to marry her! After ten whole seconds of catatonic shock, Solomon finally and joyously said, "Yes!"

Six years later, they were in a beautiful field, with their precious angels, on the best day ever. No matter how tired Solomon was, he had to spin his little girls again because he might never get another chance. No matter how hard it was for Gloria to hold back tears, she had to be strong, because her kids needed the best day ever with their daddy. No tears. Not today.

2

"You are my hiding place; you will protect me from trouble and surround me with songs of deliverance."

Psalm 32:7

"Have you seen one of those camel spiders yet? Wilson fell over the side of the road yesterday and landed in a whole pack of 'em. Freaked me out, bro."

"Dude, spiders don't go in packs. That's dogs, genius."

"Oh really? Then what do you call a 'pack' of creepy crawlies on the side of the road?"

"How the hell should I know, and why the hell should I care? But it ain't a 'pack.' "

Humvees were never made for comfort. But there can't be anything more uncomfortable than riding in the back of a Humvee, in 107-degree heat, crammed shoulder to shoulder with six pungent warriors jacked up on fear, adrenaline and phony bravado.

Private Johnson loved the sound of his own voice. He ran his mouth constantly, it seemed. But today, he took it to another level.

He was a chatterbox, pontificating on the myriad things he could do with Gomez's girlfriend; the quickest way to skin and debone a buck before the predators come; the best-tasting Skittle (purple, in case you didn't know); and, of course, Iraq's unnerving array of exotic, fist-sized spiders. Something about this little jaunt through Babylon was making Johnson extra nervous. They had done these missions before with nary a peep, but today just felt different. Sgt. Carlton was chewing his gum so fast, he was sure to get lockjaw pretty soon. Private Chenault tapped his foot as fast as the pistons under the hood.

When you're only a couple of months away from rotating back home, you get a little more nervous with each mission. Two months. Fifty-seven days. After sixteen months in this wasteland, Solomon could finally see the finish line. Sixteen months sleeping on a crappy cot alongside thirty-nine men, whom he'd come to regard as "brothers." Sixteen months coughing up beige sludge that passed for air at one time. Sixteen months dodging bullets from every direction. Sixteen months without feeling Gloria in his arms, or his children climbing over him like a jungle gym. Solomon served his country proudly for sixteen months, and now home was just fifty-seven days away.

"Where are we going this time?" Solomon asked the sergeant.

"Fallujah."

That's all he said. That's all he needed to say. Everybody knew about Fallujah. Fallujah was the place where some American troops shot up a whole bunch of unarmed Iraqis. Fallujah was the place where four U.S. mercenaries (officially called "contractors") were beaten and burned alive. They hated the U.S. with a passion in Fallujah, and the insurgency was its most virulent there. When he said "Fallujah," he could just as easily have said "hell."

Great, Solomon thought. *Another hour in this mobile slice of paradise, just to get to the worst place on earth.* He leaned his head back, closed his eyes, and tried to get a little rest.

BOOM! The shockwave from an explosion rocked the vehicle. It swerved, throwing the soldiers out of their seats and launching Johnson out the back. The vehicle skid to a halt, and they all jumped out. The lead vehicle in the convoy was engulfed in flames, and insurgents were hunkered down on the rooftops and behind the buildings, raining bullets from everywhere. Solomon set up behind the rear tire of the Humvee and started shooting up in the air, at the corner of the building, through the windows. He shot everywhere because nobody really knew where the enemy was. Well, actually they did; the enemy was *everywhere!* A casing flew up and landed inside Solomon's collar. It cooked his flesh, but he was too jacked and scared to even notice.

"Move, Trudeau!" Sgt. Carlton grabbed Solomon by the shoulder and pulled him away from the Humvee. Milliseconds later, the Humvee exploded from a rocket-propelled grenade. The blast knocked them both off their feet and left Solomon in a fog. His concussed brain decided to check out, leaving him to be carrion for the vultures. He heard nothing. He felt nothing. *Is this really happening?*

CLACK! The sound of a bullet bouncing off his helmet rattled him back into the moment. Solomon grabbed his gun and reentered the fight. *Somebody was gonna pay for this,* he thought, even though he still couldn't tell where the enemy was. As blood trickled from his ear, Solomon squeezed off round after round, not knowing if they reached their target. Then he noticed movement from the other side of the courtyard. A figure walking slowly, stealthily. He steadied himself for the attempted sneak attack that was sure to come. CLACK! Another round crackled off his helmet. Solomon did a quick barrel roll and took out an insurgent in a window!

"Booyah! Get some!" he screamed and then whirled back around to face the approaching stealthy figure. Solomon fired and hit—Johnson! The bullet tore through his chest, shattering his rib and puncturing his lung. Johnson fell to the ground in agony. Solomon was mortified.

"Johnson!" Solomon screamed and sprinted across the courtyard with reckless abandon to help his comrade. It's a miracle Solomon was not killed himself, but all he could think about was Johnson, his annoying, motor-mouth "brother."

"I'm sorry! I got you, bro," he said as he dragged Johnson behind the building.

"Got me!?" Johnson screamed. "You shot me, asshole!"

Solomon stood over Pvt. Johnson and continued the fight, but he was awash in grief over his horrible mistake. "Lord, please don't let him die. He can't die. Medic!"

AANHK AANHK AANHK AANHK AANHK. The alarm brought Solomon back from the war. His teeth were sore from grinding through the night, and his head rang from the phantom blasts of years past. He rubbed his neck where the burn from that hot shell served as a lasting reminder of what he thought at the time was his worst day ever. As if he needed a reminder. Fallujah was more than thirteen years in Solomon's rearview mirror, but he could still smell the burning gunpowder from the spent round that burned his neck as if it were being wafted under his nose like smelling salts. Thankfully, he didn't get these dreams as often anymore, not like when he first got back home. Those were some dark days and very sleepless nights.

Solomon still rose before sunrise, as if he's waking to reveille at o-dark-hundred for unit PT. In truth, he's still in the military serving on the battlefield, but he's a commissioned officer now, and his orders come from much higher up the chain. He eventually rolled out of bed to go relieve himself.

"Aim straight; shake twice," Solomon said with a bleary-eyed grin. He splashed some water on his face to stop sleepwalking, changed his shirt, and headed downstairs. His favorite room in the house was right at the bottom of the stairs, a small guest room, better suited for a child than a grown man. There are no frills or adornment for this room, just a desk, a few books and a small sofa with a couple of medium-sized throw pillows. A coat rack stands behind the door. On it hangs a black jacket, black coat, black hat and a small white strip that looks like someone folded a handkerchief down to about one inch wide. Solomon grabbed a pillow from the sofa and laid it on the floor. He closed the door, knelt down on the pillow and lowered his head to pray. Every minute he spent on his knees in the presence of the Lord pushed Fallujah, and the sleepless nights it carried, farther and farther away.

Elder Solomon Trudeau has served as a minister at Trinity Community Church (TCC) for seven years. He was raised in the church and couldn't remember a time *not* knowing that Jesus is the Son of God. Yet he never thought he would join the clergy. He felt a call to serve, but he thought he was meant to serve his country. So he enlisted in the Army a few years after he graduated from college. He had it all figured out. He would serve two years as an enlisted man and then apply to Officer Candidate School. Enlisted men make the best officers, he was told, so that was his plan. He would make lieutenant colonel by the time he was forty-six, colonel at fifty, and at least get to major general before he started thinking about retirement. Turns out, his plan wasn't His plan. God wanted Solomon in His army, not Uncle Sam's.

Solomon realized his spiritual calling back there in Fallujah as his friend lay on the ground, writhing in pain from the bullet he had fired. As he prayed for his friend and fought off the enemy, in the midst of a hail of bullets, with his ears ringing and his brain wobbly like a Jell-O mold, he heard the voice of God say, "This is not the war I need you to fight. My word is your weapon." In the middle of a firefight, with the enemy behind every nook and cranny, and his brother-in-arms struggling to survive his terrible mistake, Solomon felt a momentary sense of peace at hearing his Father's voice. Sheer terror followed at the thought of becoming a preacher! It was hard enough to be a good Christian, how on earth could he be a good preacher?!

As he reloaded his rifle, the Holy Spirit brought the words of his late father back to him: "Son, this walk of faith boils down to how you answer three simple questions: Can you hear the voice of God? Do you understand what He's telling you? And, most importantly, will you obey? If your answers ain't yes, yes and hell yeah, you're in a world o' hurt."

Solomon's dad always found a way to be equal parts Holy Ghost-filled Yoda and tobacco-spittin' country boy. Fallujah might be hell, Solomon thought, but it was infinitely better than Hell, so when he got back to the world, he traded his fatigues for a black suit, his helmet for a clergy collar, and his rifle for the Word of God.

Solomon wasn't the senior pastor, but he knew that his own church was waiting for him in the not-so-distant future. Just like when he was in the military, he had it all figured out—youth pastor for a few years, get his divinity doctorate, assistant pastor after that, then, finally, top dog. But Solomon didn't need to be the rising star right now. His immediate, most important assignment was to raise his teenage girls, and that demanded his attention most of all. So he was content to oversee the TCC Youth Ministry and do the occasional sermon, knowing his first ministry was at home. That was more than enough, in his opinion.

The sun was now up, and the smell of bacon filled the house as he emerged from The Lord's Room; there was actually a sign on the door that read "The Lord's Room." It was still quiet enough to hear Grammy's slow shuffle in the kitchen and the TSSS-TSSS-TSSS of the sprinklers. Solomon walked into the kitchen to greet the chef.

"God mornin', Mama," he said as he leaned to give her a big hug.

"God mornin', baby. Breakfast will be ready in about fifteen minutes. You have time to take a quick shower if you like."

"What are you trying to say? I stink?"

"No, baby, you don't smell. But your breath could curdle milk."

They both laughed at the good jab. A wide, thoughtful grin materialized as she caressed his cheek. Without a word, the look she gave him spoke volumes. She could sense that memories of tragic days had led to a rough night. As only a mother can, she soothed with her smile, she comforted with her gentle touch, and she strengthened with her deep, empathetic look into his soul. God really did something when he came up with mothers. Solomon trotted up the stairs to wash the night away.

Simone and Bethany were in their bathroom, brushing teeth and showering. Solomon knew it would be a good day if they weren't bickering over their shared bathroom. The two girls were totally different, but the best of friends. And even best friends disagree sometimes.

Solomon had heard horror stories about the visceral hatred that could develop between sisters. In fact, he experienced it firsthand when Sabrina Atkins asked him to the Sadie Hawkins dance in seventh grade. He accepted immediately, not because he liked her, but because he was happy someone asked him. While spastically jerking his body back and forth with Sabrina—Solomon called it "dancing," but everyone else called it hilarious—he turned around and started wiggling his nonexistent booty like a worm on a hook. When he turned back, Sabrina was on the floor being dragged by her hair! His eyes followed the braids to the hand, then up the arm, until he recognized the assailant—Tonya, her older sister. Turns out, Tonya wanted to ask him first. When Sabrina got wind of her older sister's planned sortie, she did a preemptive strike, swooping in before Tonya could engage her target. (Gloria Cooper had been there that evening, too, but she had asked Carlton Phipps. Solomon loved running into Carlton at the store now. *How you like me now, buddy?*)

The image of poor Sabrina kicking and screaming was seared into his brain. So when he saw that baby number two was another girl, he was both elated and horrified. He called his dad and told him his fears. Dad showed him the way, as only he could: "Boy,

God gave you two little angels; they just don't know it yet. It's your job to make sure they know they're little angels, not little demons. Get to work and get to prayin'." So from that day forward, Solomon whispered into their ears such thoughts as "God gave you your very own best friend," "Sisters are the best gift ever," "Your sister loves you sooooo much," "Best friends love each other at all times, even when they don't like each other." He knew a newborn and a toddler wouldn't understand, but he was speaking to their spirits. He was planting seeds that would sprout love and togetherness someday.

And it worked! Bethany and Simone were usually inseparable. If they disagreed, the hard feelings would melt away into laughter and excited little voices a few minutes later. The only thing that caused any meaningful turbulence was that bathroom. If Solomon had known, he would have scrapped all the baby-whispering and just started saving for a house with three bathrooms!

It was Saturday, and both girls had practice. Solomon always wanted his children to be athletes. He played football and ran track in college. Gloria was an awesome tennis player and could whack a golf ball almost as far as he could (but a whole lot straighter). So, the genes were there. He wasn't going the Richard Williams route—trying to raise a couple of world-dominating superstars. No, he just had one thought in mind—scholarship! They had the DNA to earn college scholarships. Gloria had been captain of the debate team and fretted every B she received, as if her very essence was being dragged into a black hole of academic ineptitude. Solomon wasn't a straight-A student, but he was a stud on the football field.

So Solomon was mortified when his first-born turned out to be a girly-girl. When he tried to teach Bethany how to bounce a basketball, she cried, "Daddy, I don't like this. The ball keeps slapping my hand, and it hurts!" When he took her to a track meet, she stared at the athletes, and he thought he had found a winner! Until she remarked, "I would never run around in the dirt all day, especially in those ugly shoes!" He even took her to a football game—not to pique her interest in that sport, but to pique her interest in *any* sport. But all she cared about were the flips and splits and dances that the cheerleaders were doing. Then it finally clicked! Solomon realized, "I have a little dancer!" So from that point on, Gloria enrolled Bethany in every dance class she could think of—jazz, ballet, tap, even salsa. She was blindly throwing darts at the wall hoping one would hit the bull's-eye—and they *all* did! Bethany's athletic genes and her prissiness found synergy on a dance floor!

But the Lord remembered Solomon, and did give him a child after his own heart. Simone was a beautiful tomboy. There wasn't a grassy hill she didn't want to roll down, a ball she didn't want to play with, or a sport she didn't want to win. She started walking two months earlier than Bethany, and Solomon made the mistake of telling her that. She began calling her big sister "Slow-Stepper." She was not only faster than Bethany, she was faster than all of Bethany's friends, including the boys. Just as Gloria took the reins over Bethany's artistic development, Solomon shepherded Simone, putting her in youth track meets by the time she was nine years old. *Scholarships, baby!*

Today, Bethany meets with her Central High dance troupe to practice for the big Tri-City Dance Competition; Simone meets with the private hurdling coach that Solomon found to help her reach her fullest potential. Coach Tim Stevenson was a renowned track-and-field coach. He actually competed in the 1984 Olympics. It was an amazing blessing to have him working with Simone. He trained only the best, and there's no way Solomon could afford his usual rate.

But Coach Stevenson had seen something in Simone even before he started working with her. He had spotted her at a local track meet and told Solomon afterward that "your little girl has got it."

"What do you mean?" Solomon replied. "She finished third. I mean, I'm proud of her, but I just don't understand why you are talking about *her* and not the winners."

Coach Stevenson explained: "The two girls who beat her today will never be as fast as what she can be. She is naturally fast, that's obvious. So are they. But your daughter has a focus that is uncommon at that age. She has a competitiveness that you can't teach. She is getting by on genes and want-to. She has no clue how to run yet. When she develops—*if* she develops—and learns how to run, she will be on a whole different level."

Solomon's chest spontaneously inflated to mammoth proportions. You could have thrown a fifty-pound dumbbell at it, and it would have ricocheted twenty feet back like a handball. Then, the pinprick of reality let all the air out. He realized he was Simone's track coach. Whatever she was or was not doing, it was because he had or had not taught her.

"Coach, do you think you can give her some pointers? I can't afford the expensive, well-coached clubs. The clubs that she has been on, I've coached or someone just as limited as me. She's literally homegrown."

"Tell you what. Bring her by the track on Tuesday at 4:30 and we'll see."

Coach Stevenson took Simone under his wing and coached her with his other athletes, without asking for a dime! "God is so good," Solomon had thought.

Solomon, Bethany, and Simone jumped into his car and headed out for their practices. The track was on the way to Central High, so Solomon decided to drop Simone off first and then continue on. It was a cloudy day, which was a blessing in Simone's mind. The temperature was at least ten degrees cooler than yesterday. No one wants to hurdle barriers *and* the heat index. When they arrived at the field, Solomon noticed the only person on the track was Coach Stevenson.

"Hmm, where is everybody?"

"I don't know, but I'm almost late. You know how Coach is if you're late. Gotta go. Love you, Daddy. Love you, Slow-Stepper." Simone winked and smiled at her big sister before sprinting down the steps to the field.

"Love you, Big Head," Bethany replied and followed with a raspberry.

HONK, HONK. Solomon waved to Coach Stevenson as he drove away.

"You know, honey," Solomon began. "What do you think about Allen Prep? I did some checking, and they have a phenomenal performing arts program. One of the teachers was an Alvin Ailey dancer."

"Daddy, why do you keep trying to get me to leave Central?" Bethany responded. "Simone's there; all my friends are there. I'm the captain of the dance troupe. And I'm a junior! Why on earth would I want to leave?"

"I just want you to have the best opportunity to not only enjoy what you love, but also be the best you can be at it. I don't want you to have any limits placed on you, even if they don't know they are putting them there."

In truth, Solomon was troubled that Simone was getting the best coaching that money didn't buy while Bethany was lumped together with a bunch of dancing daisies who didn't have one-tenth the talent of his little angel. (Yes, a father's love for his daughter can diminish all others in her orbit.)

"I was gonna surprise you, but I'll tell you now so you can chill out. Mrs. Rogers invited three members from Delta Chi Xi to the competition. That's the biggest dance fraternity in the country! One of them leads the dance troupe at UCLA and another was part of NYU's troupe."

Solomon's blood pressure started to spike. "Wait, I'm confused. What does a frat want with a seventeen-year-old girl?"

"It's a coed frat, Dad."

"Got it. Please start over. My brain locked at 'frat.' "

"Ugh! Mrs. Rogers invited some people from Delta Chi Xi, the biggest coed dance fraternity in the country. One of them leads the dance troupe at UCLA, and another was in NYU's. Anyway, Mrs. Rogers sent them video of my performance at the Bixby Theatre last summer, and they wanted to talk to me! So, see, it doesn't matter what school I'm at. If God be for me, who can stand against me? Right, Daddy?"

Solomon's chest began its involuntary inflation as he looked at his prissy little angel in the rearview mirror and nodded. "True," he said. "That's great, honey."

As the gifted dancer and awkward wiggler continued down the road, Solomon smiled and quietly thanked the Lord. *Scholarship,* he thought. His Glo-worm—the nickname was just so endearing for Solomon not to appropriate it from her father—poured so much of herself into Bethany's dancing, and it looked like it was going to reap a wonderful harvest. If only she were here to see it.

3

"Why is light given to a man whose way is hidden, and whom God has hedged in? For my sighing comes before I eat, and my groanings pour out like water. For the thing I greatly feared has come upon me, and what I dreaded has happened to me. I am not at ease, nor am I quiet; I have no rest, for trouble comes."

Job 3:23-26

If you asked Solomon, Wonder Woman masqueraded as a normal lady named Gloria Cooper Trudeau. She was smarter than everyone. She could out-athlete any woman in the state. She got a job at a big tech firm on "Innovation Alley" right out of college, and they liked her so much, they gave her a bonus after only one year! When she had Bethany—no epidural, for cryin' out loud!—she willingly left that gold mine of a job. "One of us has to raise our kids," she told Solomon. "And I want my little girl to see her daddy get up in the morning and go to work. Besides, you cook worse than you dance."

By the time Simone was one, Gloria had started an online business. Her college roommate, Ming Na, was an executive in her father's import/export business back in China. They came from two different worlds, but their spirits connected immediately. Ming didn't know the Lord, but she had a heart of gold. By the time they graduated, Gloria had led Ming to Christ, and they would be best friends for the rest of Gloria's life. She convinced Ming, who convinced her father, to sell her bulk quantities of surplus garments at a fraction of wholesale cost. Gloria resold the items through her online store. The business was so profitable, she was able to pay off her student loans in less than three years.

She truly was something! But what sealed the deal in Solomon's eyes was how she became the rock his family needed while he was off making the world safe for democracy. The day Solomon kissed her goodbye was the last time she was sad or troubled for the next eighteen months. Well, it was the last time she let him *see* her sad or troubled. Whenever he called, she was always upbeat. She would bring him up to speed on her day-to-day triumphs and stumbling blocks without the slightest hint of distress. When the kids came on the phone, they were always happy, always talking about their latest earth-shattering, monumental adventure. They would always have some question that Solomon could answer for them, which always resulted in one of them proclaiming, "You're the best daddy ever!" Even when his mom moved in just two months after he left, Gloria never gave any indication that she did so to help Gloria. According to Gloria, Grammy moved in because *she* needed support while her "baby" was off fighting on the other side of the world. Yup, Solomon was convinced he had married Wonder Woman.

Though Gloria was Wonder Woman in Solomon's eyes, she was very much human. She hid her pain, fear, anger and struggles behind a warm smile, affirming words and a confident "I got this, honey." She couldn't let him know that those eighteen months were the worst time of her young life. She couldn't let him know that she cried herself to sleep after every one of his calls. She couldn't let him know that his little girls were driving her crazy, lashing out every other week because they were mad that Daddy was gone. She couldn't let him know that the real reason Grammy moved in was because she knew her daughter-in-law needed all the help she could get. She couldn't let him know that every time their phone rang, her heart skipped a beat. Was this the call that would shatter her world into a million irreparable pieces? The call that would transform a wife into a widow? The call that would make their children fatherless?

No, Solomon couldn't know her inner struggles. He must not know. Not in the middle of a war. She couldn't have Solomon carrying any extra baggage that could weigh him down when his life was hanging in the balance. Solomon didn't need to think about anything else but doing his job and coming home. He needed to keep his mind clear, his spirit connected to His Spirit, and to come home to his family alive. She needed him to feel like the greatest husband, dad, son and soldier God ever made 'cause maybe that would make him shoot straighter, run a little faster, duck a little sooner. Maybe that would help bring him home to her. So Gloria would spend an hour in The Lord's Room before every weekly call. She would plan some fun excursion with the girls the day he called—ice cream at the pier, riding the bumper cars at Fun World, watching *Frozen* for the 217th time—so they would be too full of dopamine and serotonin to complain about anything. Gloria Cooper Trudeau was a normal lady masquerading as Wonder Woman until her husband came back to her.

It was two years after Solomon was commissioned in the army of the Lord that the myth of Wonder Woman evaporated. God turned the tables; this time it was Solomon who dreaded hearing the phone ring. Gloria's mom had passed away from lymphoma twelve years earlier. Her great-aunt had passed away from breast cancer before her fiftieth birthday. Last week, as Solomon was making love to his wife, their night of passion was shattered by the lump he felt in her breast. And now, they waited for the call that would either leave them in Neverland, or steer them into dark, uncharted territory.

RING! RING! RING! "I'm very sorry, Mrs. Trudeau. Your test came back positive for cancer. It is aggressive, so we should get you into treatment as soon as possible."

Dark territory.

Wonder Woman sank into Solomon's arms and sobbed. "I don't understand. Why me? I thought I did all the right things. I don't deserve this! No! I need to see my babies grow up. It's not fair!"

Solomon wanted to crumble into a sobbing mass on the floor, but he knew he couldn't. She needed him to be strong. *It's time for me to become her Superman.* He held her and cried with her. No words, just tears. After a long silence, he replied, "Glo-worm, God's got this. You are not gonna die! You are gonna live, and we are gonna fight together. You're gonna help plan our little girls' weddings someday. You're not done helping me become a better man. You're not done blessing people. We're gonna beat this thing. Together."

Solomon stepped up in a big way. He started taking the girls to every one of their practices. He bought four cookbooks and started cooking most of their dinners. (Eventually his mother had to move back in, because some people just can't cook, even if the directions are laid out in front of them.)

As Gloria got weaker from the chemotherapy, he would bathe her gently and carry her to bed; every so often, he would have a bubble bath prepared with rose petals, or a glass of champagne waiting on the nightstand. He knew she might be too exhausted or nauseated to partake, but if the effort warmed her heart in the midst of her struggle, it would be worth it. As her hair thinned, he would take her to shop for pretty head wraps so she could stay warm and feel beautiful at the same time. He became a clean freak, with sanitizing wipes in every room to reduce the risk of infections.

Most of all, he spent more time on his knees than ever before. Sometimes he would pray for an hour without the pillows cushioning his knees, to show God he was willing to suffer with his wife. While his wife rested, he would be in The Lord's Room seeking God's deliverance:

" 'Go into all the world and preach the gospel to all creation. Whoever believes and is baptized will be saved, but whoever does not believe will be condemned. And these signs will accompany those who believe: in My name they will drive out demons; they will speak in new tongues; they will pick up snakes with their hands; and when they drink deadly poison, it will not hurt them at all; they will place their hands on sick people, and they will get well.' Well, Lord, I'm on Your battlefield. I'm preaching Your word. I answered Your call. In the name of Jesus, I ask that You confirm Your word by the signs that accompany it. Eradicate this cancer from my wife. Let this not be unto death, but to glorify my

Lord Jesus as You restore her to health. In Jesus' name I pray. Amen."

Gloria whooped cancer's tail! She would vent (to Solomon), but she never missed a recital or parent-teacher night. She would vomit if the aroma of bacon breached her nauseated system in the morning, but she was always front and center if it was Solomon's turn in the pulpit. She might cry and ask God, "Why me?" but she would always end with "Nevertheless, thy will be done." Gloria never gave up. She never stopped fighting. But the best fighter doesn't always win. Sometimes, God's answer is "No." It was time for Gloria to go home.

Eighteen months. It was as if God were tormenting Solomon with some horribly ironic nightmare. Solomon survived a war! Bullets whizzing all around him, bombs blowing up beside him, damn camel spiders crawling all over him, and after eighteen months, he came home. His Glo-worm fought a battle against an unseen enemy that waged its assault night and day, on a battlefield just below her heart. And after eighteen months, she would never come home. An invisible mass descended upon the Trudeau family the day Gloria died, and its name was disbelief, resentment, anger. Wonder Woman was dead, and the countless hours Solomon had spent on his knees praying, or on his feet preaching, didn't make a difference. From that day forward, every lesson he taught had a little less fire; every sermon he preached had a little less conviction; and every prayer he prayed had a little less faith behind it.

At her funeral, Pastor Jefferson gave Solomon a big, long hug. He stepped to the podium and delivered a stirring eulogy, hitting all the right notes: "Gloria was a true light in darkness." "Gloria is better off now than we are—she's home with Jesus, praising God." "No day is promised, so while our hearts break that we do not have our dear sister with us, let us rejoice that the Lord shared one of His angels with us for thirty-six years."

It was a comforting eulogy, an encouraging eulogy. It lifted everyone's heart—everyone's but Solomon's. As he tried to cope, one question kept creeping into his mind: *Did I fail my wife?* But there was no time for that. Solomon had two little girls who needed him—now, more than ever. They needed Superman to come save the day.

4

"Be sober, be vigilant; because your adversary the devil walks about like a roaring lion, seeking whom he may devour."

1 Peter 5:8

"Hey, Coach!" Simone yelled, as she stepped away from the car. Coach was fanatical about punctuality. A late arrival would cost her at least two extra sprints at the end of practice. "Five minutes early is ten minutes late!" he would say. Practice starts at 9:30 a.m. —two minutes from now.

"Cuttin' it close, young lady," Coach Stevenson said with a jokingly menacing stare. "Go ahead and get warmed up."

"Whew," Simone sighed in relief. "Coach must be in a good mood today."

Coach Tim Stevenson was a lean, forty-seven-year-old man who looked like he could still run a ten-second hundred-meter dash. He competed in masters meets all the time, almost always finishing in the top two. Running would not be an appropriate description of what he does on the track. Some runners are muscle-driven pistons that beat the track (and the other racers) into submission. Those runners are Corvettes, because they almost always huff and bark and growl to hype themselves up before a race, like a Corvette at a red light. Some runners are long, with strides that take seconds to return to the ground. Those runners are cheetahs, because they spend more time in the air than their prey. Coach Stevenson was different. Every step springs from the ground with incomprehensible power yet almost balletic gentleness. His legs are long like a Cheetah's, but his turnover is quick like a Corvette. Coach Stevenson doesn't run—he glides. With such a beautiful gait, and such a beautiful physique, and with such deep understanding of the very essence of running, it's no surprise at all that sixteen-year-old Simone Trudeau had a crush on him. And being such a well-traveled ladies' man, it's no surprise that he recognized it the second they met.

"Where is everybody, Coach?" Simone asked as she finished her warm-up laps.

"I gave them some cross-training work today. They're running a couple miles through Crow Neck Canyon," Coach replied.

"Why didn't you let me go with them? I can cross-train!" Being the youngest in the group, but the most competitive, Simone was hypersensitive to any inkling that she couldn't keep up, always fearful in the back of her mind that today might be the day when Coach would cut her loose.

"I know, but you need more work on technique at this stage. Cross-training will come when I see your technique catch up to your speed. Besides, some days I just want to be selfish and not share that pretty little smile with anyone else." Like that, all of Simone's worry melted away into a huge, toothy, bashful smile. If Coach Stevenson decided to become a politician, he'd glide to victory there, too.

"Alright, let's stretch," he said. Simone got down on the ground and spread her legs nearly 180 degrees. Coach Stevenson knelt behind her, gently pushed her down to the right, and held her in that position.

"Ahh! Damn wrist is killing me. Started acting up yesterday. I'm gettin' old." Coach Stevenson slid in closer to use his forearms to push Simone forward.

"Ouch! Coach, your elbow is digging into my back."

"Crap. Sorry about that. We'll make this thing work."

Coach Stevenson leaned his torso forward and pressed his perfect chest against her back to hold her in the stretched position. Simone said nothing, but her mind was alight! Synapses firing. Hormones racing. She had *never* felt like this before. She was both exhilarated and terrified. Usually she hated stretching. She wanted to get it over with as soon as possible so she could hit the track. Today was different. Today, she held each position a little bit longer. Coach Stevenson took full notice. His elbow started to poke her in the back again, but she refused to say a word. She couldn't ruin this moment for a lousy prod in the back.

"OK," Coach Stevenson said. "Turn over."

Simone rolled over to her back and lifted one leg straight up in the air. Coach Stevenson knelt on one knee, rested her raised calf against his chest, locked her leg in place with his arm and her other leg with his foot, then slowly leaned forward.

"Lower . . . lower," Simone directed, as the coach pressed her leg forward with his chest in response. "Stop."

Coach Stevenson's chest was two feet from the very limber girl. Simone stared intently, excited to tell her sister about the best day ever! Coach stared off into the distance, his gold cross dangling to within inches of Simone's face.

"Reset." Coach lifted back up and started the stretch all over again.

"Lower . . . lower . . . lower . . . lower." She was close enough to hear his heartbeat, close enough to smell his cologne (*Cologne, at the track! What a man!* her naive mind thought), close enough to feel his—*Wait, is that his cell phone?* The hard poke couldn't be his forearm this time. *Yeah, cell phone or his keys,* she reasoned within herself. Then slowly, purposefully, Coach Stevenson turned his head down and looked directly into Simone's bewildered, innocent eyes and gave a telling grin that screamed, "You know exactly what that is." At that moment, Simone understood for the first time the saying "the eyes are the windows to one's soul." She gazed deep into Coach Stevenson's eyes and saw—nothing! No love, no goodness, no mercy. It was a dark, lustful, prideful chasm. Her best day ever had morphed into a nightmare—alone, pinned beneath a highly aroused predator, and it was hungry.

"Coach, you can let me up now."

Silence. The predator maintained its paralyzing hold and intent gaze. It grinned and, with a voice that Simone didn't recognize, it said, "know you want me. I want you. Let me make you a woman today."

"No, Coach. Please let me up."

The predator didn't say a word. A smile, sinister enough to bring chills, told Simone her "Coach" was long gone. She froze.

Solomon had taught Bethany and her a few moves to protect themselves or break away from somebody, but what move is there when a 180-pound man has one leg pinned to the ground, the other leg pinned to his chest, and an erection just a few millimeters of fabric away from stealing her innocence?

As panic began to set in, Simone closed her eyes and prayed before she began the fight of her life. *Lord, help me!* her soul cried out in a spiritual roar that shook heaven into action. Then, peace. A calm enveloped her. She opened her eyes and gave the predator a subtle smile and an approving wink. It gave a devilish smile and then reached down to undo its pants. As it prepared to rape young Simone Trudeau, the predator relaxed its grip and concentration just enough for Simone to see the way of escape the Lord had provided. With her arm free and its attention elsewhere, she raised her thumb and thrust her hand upward, poking it in the eye. The predator yelped in pain, but it didn't have time to grab its injured cornea, because without hesitation, Simone grabbed its esophagus, squeezed and twisted. The predator crumbled in pain as Simone pushed him off of her and ran as fast as she could.

But the predator could still glide. It effortlessly caught up to the terrified teenager and grabbed her from behind, covering her mouth with its paw. She couldn't see its face this time, but she didn't need to, to know what the eyes of the predator were saying now—rage, retribution, evil. She kicked and flailed, but to no avail, her screams muffled by its sweaty, dirty paws.

Then, yet again, peace. She stopped kicking, stopped flailing. The Holy Spirit brought a distant memory back to the forefront of her mind. In a flash, Simone remembered what her father had taught her years ago. It was in their front yard. Solomon told the girls to come outside because he wanted to show them something. When they came out, they didn't see him. Suddenly, Solomon grabbed Bethany from behind and held her tight. She screamed like her life depended on it, but he didn't' let go. He calmly said, "Now, get out of it."

Bethany cried, "I can't!" and tears flowed down her beautiful face. Simone stood there completely catatonic, her mind unable to reconcile the scene that was unfolding.

"Relax, baby. It's Daddy," Solomon said, as he released his petrified little girl. "I will never hurt you, but I can't say the same for many of the guys in this fallen world, especially if they've been drinking. Don't say you can't; just ask me to teach you how." For the next thirty minutes, they practiced escape moves. Every so often, they would practice these moves—including striking the most sensitive and vulnerable spots to temporarily or permanently neutralize an attacker—until Solomon was confident that his little girls knew enough to get away from a pissed-off ex-boyfriend or angry husband—or a predator.

Simone felt her power again. It had never left, but panic had made her forget, for a moment, who she was and Whose she was. She put her hand on the paw covering her mouth and dug her nails into its flesh. She grabbed its hair with her other hand and yanked hard enough to ensure a bald spot would announce to the world that Simone Trudeau will not be a victim today! With quick, fluid motions, she poked its other eye with her thumb, threw her elbow into its ribs, and grabbed its paw. Then she lifted her knees and flung her feet out and down to the ground, while thrusting her derriere into its abdomen and pulling forward on its paw, sending the predator tumbling head over heels onto its back. She stomped its still-erect member, then jumped as high as she could and landed with as much force as her 140-pound frame could muster, squarely onto its knee. The satisfying *pop* she heard told her this glider was now permanently grounded. As the predator screamed, cursed and writhed in pain, Simone grabbed her bag and ran. She stopped at his car to let the air out of one of its tires to make sure this predator didn't get away. Then, she reached into her bag, pulled out her phone, and dialed Superman.

Solomon had meant to return to the track immediately after dropping Bethany off—his papa-bear instincts told him this needed to be a quick turnaround. As soon as he walked Bethany into the gymnasium, though, he ran into Sister Janet Strickland. Sister Janet was a member of the TCC congregation, and her daughter had attended his Sunday school class. Her daughter was also on the same dance team with Bethany. The two exchanged pleasantries, but Solomon knew it couldn't extend any longer than a minute.

As it turned out, he had even less time than that. Right after the two hugged, Simone called with her horrifying cry for help: "Daddy, help! Please come quick! Coach just tried to rape me!" The absolute horror of those words catapulted Solomon into a nebula of uncontrollable emotions, but now wasn't the time for him to figure them out. No, all he needed to do was go save his little girl. Solomon asked Janet to take Bethany home after practice. He knew her and trusted her, so he knew Bethany would be safe. Janet knew Solomon and, in her heart of hearts, wanted to know more of him. She agreed without hesitation, and without grasping the gravity of the situation until Solomon turned and sprinted out the gym. He was already gone when she closed her eyes, lifted her hand toward the door, and whispered, "Lord, whatever is going on, please cover Pastor Trudeau. Send Your angel with him to guide him to wherever he's going. Go before

Your servant and touch the situation, right now, in Jesus' name. Amen. Be careful, Solomon."

"I'm running to the car, and I'll be there in ten minutes. Where is he?"

"He's still on the track trying to get up. It was so horrible, Daddy. Please hurry!"

"Drop your bag, keep your phone, and start running. Call the police. Tell 'em what happened and to meet you at the Rite Aid on Winnetka. Stay on the phone with them. I'll be right there."

Solomon jumped in his car and gunned it. The trip was usually a twenty-minute drive, but there was nothing that would stop him from doing at least ninety miles per hour. Now that he was racing to his little girl, his mind descended deep into that nebula.

There was rage: *I will kill him with my bare hands!*

Guilt: *Why did I leave my little girl there? Alone! What was I thinking?!*

Panic: *My God! My baby needs me, and I'm twenty minutes away!*

Denial: *It can't be. Not my little girl. No, please just be a horrible joke.*

Confusion: *How can one man get the worst phone call imaginable* twice *in one lifetime?*

More Confusion: *What did she mean by 'he's trying to get up'?*

And Fear: *What if he catches up to her before she can get to the drugstore?*

Simone dialed 9-1-1 and told them everything she could while sprinting to the Rite Aid. The drugstore was about a four-hundred-meter dash away from the track, but on the way, Simone spotted a police car in the parking lot of the Crossroads Diner. "Thank you, Jesus! I gotta go; there's a cop here," In the midst of her adrenaline-filled flight, she instinctively hung up the phone and detoured into the diner. She ran up to the officer, who was enjoying coffee and breakfast before his shift began.

"Help me, please. My coach just attacked me!"

Officer Mark Donnelly scanned the frantic little girl and knew she wasn't playing a prank. "Are you hurt, miss?" Her elbows were a bit bloody from scraping the ground. Her hair was disheveled. There was a mark on the side of her mouth that could have come from a finger or two pressed against it. And her eyes screamed, "Save me!"

"No, sir. I . . . I don't think so."

Officer Donnelly stood up and took Simone outside. "OK. Miss, what is your name?"

"S-S-Simone Trudeau." She started to shiver uncontrollably.

"How old are you?"

"S-s-sixteen."

"You're safe now, Simone. I won't let anyone hurt you. Please tell me what happened. Who—" Officer Donnelly stopped as Simone crumbled into a sobbing heap. Hearing him say "you're safe" allowed her to exhale for what felt like the first time in thirty minutes. And with that exhale, she could stop fighting and just cry.

"It's OK, Simone. Who did this to you?"

"Coach," she eked out in between sobs.

"Coach who?"

"Coach Tim Stevenson. He's my track coach."

"Where is he now?"

"I left him at the track."

"OK." Officer Donnelly grabbed his radio. "Adam 412. Dispatch, over."

"Dispatch. Adam 412. What's your status?"

"I gotta girl here reporting an assault over at the track on Carlson and Route 10. Perp might still be there. Name is Tim Stevenson. Request immediate backup to go check it out. I'm staying with the girl until y'all give me the all clear at the track."

"Copy that, Adam 412. Units are already in route. 911 dispatched 'em two minutes ago. Will let you know when the scene is secure."

"Roger that."

"Simone, we're on it. We will get this guy, don't you worry."

Officer Donnelly motioned toward the waitress, who was staring through the window—along with everyone else in the diner —and beckoned for her to come. Her face grew pale as she pressed her hand against her chest as if to say "Me?" He waved her outside, and she complied, skittishly. "Can you please bring this young lady a hot chocolate." The waitress instantly relaxed, relieved that she was not being brought any deeper into the situation. She nodded "Will do," and headed back inside.

"OK, Simone, I need you to tell me what happened at the track."

Solomon arrived at the Rite Aid and screeched to a halt, toppling over some grocery carts.

"Simone!" he screamed as he jumped out of the car. He couldn't see her anywhere. He ran into the drugstore and screamed her name again, running up and down the aisles. The manager confronted him, saying, "Sir, may I help you?"

"My daughter, Simone. She's in trouble, and I told her to meet me here. Have you seen her?"

"Not that I know of, sir. Do you have a picture?" Solomon

pulled out his phone and showed him a photo of Simone.

"No, sir, but let's ask April. She's been working the register nearest the door for the last hour. If anyone here has seen your daughter, it would be her."

The manager took Solomon over to the cashier and showed her the photo. "No, I haven't seen her come in."

Solomon's head started to spin. "No, please no, Lord." His worst nightmare seemed to be coming to fruition. *Did Coach catch her before she could get here? Did he take my little girl?* He pulled his phone out to call, but to his dismay, found it completely out of power. Solomon jumped back in his car and headed to the track, praying that Simone was OK.

When he pulled up to the track, he saw two police cruisers parked, lights flashing. "Dear God, no, no, please no." He jumped out of his car, but in his frenzied state, he put the car in neutral instead of park. The car idled forward and came to rest on the driver-side door of the cruiser. Solomon ran to the top of the stairs and saw the police handcuffing Coach Stevenson, but where was Simone?

"Where's my little girl!" Solomon screamed, as he sprinted toward Coach Stevenson with murderous intentions. The police tackled him to the ground just steps before he crushed the perp.

"Where is she?!"

"Sir, please calm down," an officer said. "Your daughter is safe. She's with an officer. I'll ask him to bring her here now. Please, just calm down."

She's safe. Thank God, she's safe.

5

"You shall not hate your brother in your heart. You shall surely rebuke your neighbor, and not bear sin because of him. You shall not take vengeance, nor bear any grudge against the children of your people, but you shall love your neighbor as yourself: I am the Lord."

Leviticus 19:17-18

Solomon closed the door after leaving The Lord's Room. As he walked away, he stopped and turned back. Looking at the sign above the door, he muttered, "Where are you?"

It's been eleven months since that terrible day at the track, but it all ends today. Today, Solomon and Simone have to face her attempted rapist one more time. Today, Simone gets to confront the man who tried to take her purity, the man who stole the same from so many others, and let him know with her own voice that he did not, could not and will never take her power away from her. Her voice shall be heard today, justice shall be met, and peace shall return to Solomon's soul—or so he hoped.

Something was different for Solomon. The power in his praise was diminished; the fervency of his prayer evaporated; and the

Light within that once shone brightly was now obscured by the cloud of emotions that he had yet to reconcile. Fitful nights were now commonplace, as the ghosts of tragedies past haunted his dreams. So, instead of leaving his spiritual fortress of solitude empowered, invigorated and steadfast, Solomon left The Lord's Room the same way he entered: disconnected. "Where are you?"

When the news got out about the Olympian-turned-coach-turned-predator, more and more girls and women came forward to tell their stories of innocence stolen by Coach Tim Stevenson. Like any predator, he searched for his prey at the known watering holes; that meant he would go to local prep track meets under the guise of scouting for hidden gems he could help mold into the next great phenom. Like any predator, he would find the weakest target and then isolate it from the herd; that meant using his Olympic pedigree and professed Christian faith to gain the trust of the prey's parents. Like any predator, he stalked his prey and waited for the opportune moment to pounce; that meant ensuring no one else would be on the track that day so he could devour his meal without interruption.

The portrait of a monster was painted with every story. He would teach them as he groomed them. He would pray with them, as he preyed on them. As his stock as a coach increased, the age of his prey decreased. He found his targets as minors but was usually careful to wait until after their seventeenth or eighteenth birthday before consummating his lustful intentions. And he had never been violent before—not until Simone Trudeau fought back. All the victims had been stalked so skillfully, groomed so surreptitiously, that when he struck, they capitulated, then held their secret in silence. Some thought he cared for them so much it was no big deal. Some felt ashamed as they confused naïve infatuation with consent. Those who said no in the moment, felt afraid that exposing a living legend would destroy their own dreams of running for gold. They all had their reasons for keeping silent, but like Simone, they all shared one common trait: they were the survivors of a sexual predator.

But there was only one who fought back. Until then, this predator was able to hide behind the mask of Coach Tim Stevenson, a trusted, Christian, track god, because no one ever fought back. His prey had always surrendered to his cunning and patient pursuit. Simone exposed the animal behind the mask when her thumb met its cornea. No predator gives up on a long-stalked meal easily; neither would Tim Stevenson give up on his prey easily. But Tim Stevenson miscalculated. The effervescent teenager with a crush on her famous coach was herself masking a Power that he didn't know was there, even though he professed to be endued with the same. Wonder Woman was back, and her name was Simone Trudeau.

But Wonder Woman was just a sixteen-year-old girl who was forced to face evil far too early. Simone had won the battle that day, but she was left to fight her way out of a pit of fear, depression, mistrust and anger. *What did I do wrong? Did I lead him on? What if I hadn't been able to fight him off that day? Who can I trust?*

For seven months after the attack, Simone saw the world through tear-filled eyes. She stopped running, which was her first love. She stopped smiling, which used to light up the room, braces and all. Her grades slipped. But one thing that never wavered was her faith. She never blamed God. A couple of weeks after the attack, a kind soul at church came to her and just hugged her.

There was such tenderness, such empathy in that hug that she started to cry even though no words were spoken. Sister Janet Strickland just held her like a mother would hold her broken daughter, trying to mend the pieces back together with love. After the loving silence, Sister Strickland whispered into Simone's ear, "I don't know why that happened to you, baby, but it will not destroy you. Don't let it define you either. 'All things work together for good to them that love God and who are the called according to His purpose.' Don't ask God, 'Why me?' Just ask Him to show you the good. He will, in His time."

From that day forward, Simone attacked that question "show me the good" the way she attacked each hurdle. She discovered The Lord's Room—until then, it had just been "that room that Daddy prays in"—and spent the time that she would have been running, in His Room searching for the Scripture, and others like it, that Sis Strickland had told her. She found herself on her knees more in the months following the attack than in her whole life. *Please God, show me the good.*

Three days before the trial of State vs. Timothy O. Stevenson began, the Lord sent Simone the answer. A number of the survivors had contacted the district attorney's office in an effort to reach out to her. Because she was a minor, the D.A. refused to give her information but forwarded their requests on to Solomon. Solomon was hesitant at first but eventually contacted one of the victims, Ms. Sherrie Walker.

"Hi, Ms. Walker. My name is Solomon Trudeau. The district attorney's office said you would like to talk to my daughter."

"My God!" Sherrie blurted out. "Thank you for getting back to me. Yes, I would. How is she?"

"She's a fighter, ma'am, but this isn't a fight a little girl should have to wage. It's a struggle, but we'll pull through. Why do you want to speak with her?"

"Glory to God. I pray for her every day, Mr. Trudeau. It's not just me that wants to speak with her. All of us do," she said.

"Us?" Solomon asked, perplexed.

"Yes. The survivors of Tim Stevenson. We want to meet with your daughter to let her know she isn't alone."

"Ma'am, she knows. Everyone knows. Please forgive me, but I don't remember your name as one of the past victims."

Sherrie took a deep breath and replied: "I am twenty-nine years old now and raising a son on my own. I chose to keep my name, and family, out of the papers, Mr. Trudeau. But when I heard what happened to your daughter, it struck me to the core. I never realized he was a predator. I just thought that he was a player who took advantage of an eighteen-year-old girl—a girl who was a little too fast off the track, if you know what I mean. I know the news has spread far and wide that Simone isn't alone, but that doesn't make her feel any less isolated. I feel it in my spirit, Mr. Trudeau, that she needs to hear it from us. She needs to feel the love from us. She needs to receive the admiration from us. She needs to know that, to us, she is a hero."

Silence. Solomon wasn't contemplating; he was crying. After a few moments, he wiped away his tears and said, "Let's make it happen."

So, two weeks into the trial, Solomon loaded his family—Grammy, Bethany and Simone—into the car and told them, "We have to go meet some people for the trial." Only Grammy knew the real purpose; they were going to meet the other survivors. In fact, it was Grammy's idea to keep it a secret. With sage wisdom, she told him, "Son, my baby needs this, but she don't need the anxiety that'll come from thinking about it."

When they got to the district attorney's office, Grammy and Bethany hopped in the elevator, but Solomon and Simone took the stairs. Ever since the day of the attack, Simone couldn't be in confined spaces. The trauma was always there now, fear slowly metastasizing into every area of her life. Solomon and Grammy could see it happening but couldn't stop it. It would take an act of God to save his little girl from a lifetime of fear, broken dreams and unfulfilled promise. After about five minutes, they emerged from the eleventh-floor stairwell. The Trudeaus embraced outside the office, and Grammy said a short prayer for them before they entered.

"Good morning," said the receptionist cheerfully. "How may I help you?"

"Hi. The Trudeaus here to see D.A. Rosenfeld."

"Please have a seat, and I'll let him know you're here."

The D.A. came out and greeted them warmly. He escorted them to a pair of large, wooden double doors. Then he paused and looked at Simone, who looked sullen and mortified that she would have to relive that terrible day again. He said, "Young lady, today isn't about *that* day. Today is about the rest of your life. There are some people who would like to help you look forward, not backward." He swung the door open, revealing a medium-sized conference room filled with women. They turned, saw Simone, and spontaneously began to clap and cry. People in the D.A.'s office, who were privy to what was to take place, had quietly gathered behind the Trudeaus to witness the moment. They also began to clap and wipe away tears. Even D.A. Rosenfeld had to turn his head and feign a cough to collect himself. Simone's eyes grew wide, and she froze. Ms. Sherrie Walker stepped forward and hugged her close. She whispered, "God has heard you, sweetie. You are not alone. You are our hero and we are 'the good.' " They hugged for an eternity, their souls intertwining into a lifelong bond of faith, hope and love. As the tears flowed, the Trudeaus walked into the conference room, and young Simone Trudeau was inundated with more love, admiration and encouragement than she could have imagined.

Simone emerged from this divine intervention a new woman. She held her head a little higher; her shoulders, farther back; and her walk, a lot less tepid. She started down the stairs out of habit, but then she remembered what Sherrie had told her in the room: "You are more than a conqueror because your strength is in Christ, and no man can take that strength from you!" She took Solomon's hand, left the stairwell and walked to the elevators. She pushed the down button and watched the numbers as each one lit up, edging closer to her floor.

At first, she squeezed Solomon's hand. *My little girl has quite a grip.* Solomon winced silently.

Ninth floor—she grabbed his arm and squeezed.

Sixth floor—she closed her eyes and whimpered, "Daddy."

Ding. The doors opened. She opened her eyes, and her fear melted away. God had sent an angel. Ms. Sherrie Walker stood alone in the elevator. She opened her arms to the scared little girl. Simone stepped forward into her warm embrace. Solomon followed and put his arms around both women. As the elevator doors closed, Simone's heart began to bloom once more.

One heart opened as another remained bound. Solomon was happy for the breakthrough his daughter had experienced that day. But it didn't curb the anger that burned within him. That anger grew as he sat day after day and faced the monster that attacked his little girl and heard the gut-wrenching details of not just that day, but all the other days he violated innocence. The anger grew as he listened and realized he had been groomed almost as much as his daughter. Why else would he have left his baby girl alone on a field with a forty-seven-year-old man? Why else would he ignore his inner alarm that screamed, "Where is everyone?"

The anger grew as he thought about all he had endured for the Lord—his military career, the meager means of a reverend, hours on his knees praying for Gloria, countless Sunday school lessons and sermons—and yet, the Lord still took his Glo-worm, and the Lord still introduced his little girl to a monster. Solomon hoped today would finally bring him peace. He hoped seeing that monster led away in chains for the last time would finally close that chapter and set him free. Free to be who he used to be. Free to experience God's presence like he used to.

By some awful twist of fate, the sentencing hearing wasn't the only sobering task on Solomon's plate this day. The father of his boyhood friend had passed ten days earlier, and today was the funeral. Solomon was the obvious choice to officiate, and he wholeheartedly accepted. When he got the call that the sentencing hearing had been moved to the same day, there was nothing he could do. He couldn't neglect his friend during his time of grief or his duties as a minister of the gospel of Jesus Christ. He was just thankful that the hearing was late enough in the afternoon for him to accomplish both.

The funeral for Walter Johnson was an understated affair. He was an occasional congregant at TCC, so a few of the parishioners were present to pay their respects. Pastor Solomon Trudeau wore his official clergy uniform—his coat of armor, he used to call it—and delivered a rather thoughtful and reflective eulogy. People cried, amens were heard throughout, and the deceased was remembered. Yet, the Power was missing—and Solomon knew it. *I'm just preoccupied with the hearing,* he thought. *Once I get past this, it will all be over. I'll get my head clear and get back to being me,* he told himself. One of the attendees, Sister Strickland, approached him as he tried to break away.

"Pastor, that was a wonderful message," she said, and to her it was, only Solomon knew otherwise.

"Thank you, Sister Strickland. I must be going now. Gotta get to the courthouse."

"I know, Pastor. 'The Lord bless you and keep you; the Lord make His face shine upon you, and be gracious to you; the Lord lift up His countenance upon you, and give you peace.' "

"Thank you, Sister."

As Solomon tried to pull away, Sister Strickland held onto his hand and handed him a small envelope.

"Please, Pastor, hold onto this card. Don't open it now. Take it to the hearing today and open it there, if you feel an unction to do so."

"I will. Thank you."

The courthouse was only ten minutes away, but the Trudeaus lived nearly thirty minutes away. Solomon didn't have time to go home, change clothes and get to the courthouse in time. So there he was, next to his little girls in a courtroom—they had taken the bus—fully suited in his clerical coat of armor, though he removed his clergy collar so he could loosen the neck on his shirt.

The court was packed with other survivors, their families, some reporters and a few bystanders who just wanted to be there. An elderly woman was sitting directly in front of Bethany. Solomon had seen her before; she attended every hearing. She was the defendant's mother and lone supporter, Cora Stevenson.

There were three other women there to face Tim Stevenson and tell him what was on their heart. Simone was the last to speak. As each woman came forward, their words of condemnation, victory and empowerment were a triumph over evil that touched everyone —everyone but the defendant, it seemed. Tim Stevenson sat there stone-faced. There was no regret, no contrition, no empathy. He looked each woman in the eye throughout her entire statement but never betrayed even the faintest hint of sorrow for his actions. Nor did he seem to accept that he was the predator his accusers, the jury, the judge and society in general said he was. Solomon seethed inside. Turning the small envelope around and around in his hands, he thought: *Five minutes. Just five minutes alone with that guy.*

6

"Yet in all these things we are more than conquerors through Him who loved us. For I am persuaded that neither death nor life, nor angels nor principalities nor powers, nor things present nor things to come, nor height nor depth, nor any other created thing, shall be able to separate us from the love of God which is in Christ Jesus our Lord."

Romans 8:37-39

Since the day they met, Simone and Sherrie spoke every week, sometimes just for a few minutes, sometimes for over an hour. They developed a deep, spiritual sisterhood that could only be Providence. Turns out, Sherrie had been a budding track star ten years, one child and a few pounds ago. They shared stories of past and present triumphs, stories of little girl crushes, and even stories of how Tim Stevenson had altered the course of their lives. When Simone found peace and comfort in Sherrie's motherly embrace as those elevator doors closed, her spirit knew the Lord had listened to her and would continue to listen to her, as long as she continued to open the door of her heart to Him. So one thing always remained constant in their conversations: prayer. No matter how short or how long the conversation was, Simone and Sherrie would always welcome the Holy Spirit in and pray over their lives.

Sherrie became both Simone's friend and spiritual mother. She would give Simone thought-provoking scriptures to read and pray over and Christ-centered advice on whatever matters were on her heart. As time passed, Simone became bolder, stronger, more confident in who she was, because she truly began to understand Whose she was. Sherrie even helped her figure out what to say to Tim Stevenson. Well, Simone knew *what* she wanted to say, but Sherrie helped her figure out how to say it.

When Simone's time came to address the court, she wasn't the scared little girl who sat on the witness stand a few months earlier. That day in the conference room was like the first rays of spring sun shining on the closed petals of a lily in the field. She had an epiphany that many full-grown Christians never realize: God's love and divine plan included her! God could turn the worst thing that ever happened to her into a testimony of overwhelming power. She no longer felt shame for her innocent emotions; she felt determined to be the example of perseverance and Godly character that those other women saw in her, and helped her see in herself. And now, eleven months after the predator in Tim Stevenson tried to destroy her with its evil inclinations, she rose up, unfolded her carefully prepared statement and proceeded to let her enemy know *she* had won.

"Your Honor," she began, "thank you for this opportunity to address the court and Mr. Stevenson. Mr. Stevenson, last year you tried to take something priceless from me. I'm not referring to my virginity, though I'm sure that's what your corrupt mind was thinking. Though it is also priceless, and something I could never get back—something I promised God, and my father, that I would preserve for the one He sends—what you tried to steal is even more valuable: my self-worth, my self-respect, my self-confidence, my peace, my faith. You tried to rob me of who I am as a woman. You tried to rob me of what makes me, *me*!

"You probably don't even get what I'm talking about. The fact that you have chosen to plead not guilty tells me you don't understand the gravity of your thefts. In your mind, we were all 'women' who got what they 'wanted' deep down inside. In your mind, it was just sex, something everyone wants. In your mind, every single 'No' you heard was the real lie, because to you, our eyes were screaming 'Yes.' You didn't say these things, but it's written all over your face. You never accepted responsibility for what you stole, or tried to steal, because you don't even realize you're a thief, and a pawn. So, let me help you understand.

"Puberty does not mean we are women. Not even our eighteenth birthday means we are full-grown. We are still girls trying to grow up, trying to figure out who to trust. We are counting on adults to show us the way until we are mature enough to find it on our own. You stole a priceless piece from every single girl you violated. When you took advantage of your role and our innocence, you chipped a piece of trust and peace from our hearts and stuck it on your belt like a notch.

"It's never 'just sex,' Mr. Stevenson. Even if the woman is thirty years old, it can't be 'just sex.' Women are not like men, Mr. Stevenson. Every time a man enters a woman, she gives a piece of her very being to him, and she leaves the encounter a little less whole if he doesn't cherish that piece for what it is—her heart, her hopes.

"Eyes are the windows to one's soul, but eyes do not speak, Mr. Stevenson! What part of the word "No" is so difficult to understand? A woman can have a thousand conflicting emotions going on at the same time, but all you should care about are the words that come out of her mouth. 'No' means 'No,' Mr. Stevenson. Anything after that is called rape.

"You were a coach. People put their futures in your hands. We trusted you to bring out the best in us, to help us be the best we could possibly be at the sport we loved. You took advantage of our trust, our faith in you, our naiveté and our admiration.

"So I hope you understand why this court has proven you guilty, why so many people are calling you a monster, and why so much anger is directed toward you. But, you're not my enemy, Mr. Stevenson. 'We do not wrestle against flesh and blood, but against principalities, against powers, against the rulers of the darkness of this age, against spiritual hosts of wickedness in the heavenly places.' You are a pawn, Mr. Stevenson. You wore your cross so proudly, but, remember, even the devils believe and tremble. Against my real enemy, who has used you to steal from so many women, used you to destroy, or try to destroy, so many lives, including your own, I will fight with the one weapon it can't deny or withstand. The thief does not come except to steal and to kill and to destroy. Jesus came so I may have life, and that I may have it more abundantly. Enemy, you tried and failed. If you try again, you will fail again. I am more than a conqueror through Christ who loves me! You will not steal my peace, you will not kill my dreams, and you will not destroy my future, because I know who I am and who my Father is. I can do all things through Christ who gives me strength! You made a big mistake coming after me. Just as I defeated your pawn on that field, I will defeat you for the rest of my life. The stone you tried to toss on the trash heap of life shall become a cornerstone of faith! I dedicate my life to building my Lord's kingdom and destroying yours.

"I forgive you, Mr. Stevenson. I will not allow the enemy to take up any more of my time, energy and peace. For me, this ends today. Now!"

Simone folded the sheet of paper as tears flowed down her cheeks. She didn't want her attacker, or anyone watching, to think her tears belied her triumph, her resolve, her peace. So she looked back at Tim Stevenson and said, "These are not tears of pain. These are tears of joy. I am victorious! Not because I was able to fight you off. No, I have victory because I am free. And my journey is just beginning. Your freedom has ended, Mr. Stevenson, but I don't want you to rot in prison. That would be a waste of a life. The gifts God put in you when you were in your mother's womb are irrevocable. It would be a shame for them to be wasted. Reflect, repent and be reborn before it's too late, Mr. Stevenson."

Simone returned to her seat, with her head held high. The court erupted in spontaneous applause for the powerful teenager. As the judge slammed her gavel down to restore order, Solomon stood and welcomed her with a big, long hug. For a moment, immeasurable pride and, of all things, admiration replaced his rage. He was stunned at the mighty woman of God that his little girl had morphed into. He was astounded by her words, her power. And he knew the Source, because he used to have that same faith, that same power. The preacher was awestruck, hoping he would be as strong as his little girl someday.

As he and Simone took their seats again, Solomon returned his gaze to Tim Stevenson and saw, for the first time, *something*. The stone face wasn't as rigid. His posture was a bit less proud. His eyes, not as resolute. Solomon's little girl had gotten through. Solomon felt it was time to open the envelope now. He pulled it from his pocket, not realizing almost half his clergy collar came out with it. Sister Strickland had written a single Bible verse: "Then Peter came to Him and said, 'Lord, how often shall my brother sin against me, and I forgive him? Up to seven times?' Jesus said to him, 'I do not say to you, up to seven times, but up to seventy times seven.' " The words clawed at his heart, even as they tasted like castor oil in his mouth. *Forgive. I know I need to. Lord, please help me forgive.* Solomon looked up from the paper to see if he could find that sliver of humanness in Tim Stevenson's eyes once more. *Help me see that again. Help me.*

The coach was looking in their direction. This time his eyes were warm and focused on his weeping mother, seated right in front of Bethany. He couldn't console his mother physically, so he did what he used to do when she would watch him from the stands at his competitions: he gave her a reassuring smile and a disarming wink.

Solomon was incensed. *He just smiled and winked at Bethany!* Tim Stevenson was taunting the one daughter he assaulted by having the audacity to flirt with the other daughter he didn't have a chance to stalk. To Solomon, he was dismissing Simone's—and every other survivor's—words with the same charisma he used to secure their confidence—and his.

"You son of a bitch!" Rev. Solomon Trudeau screamed at the former coach. He crumpled the card in his hands and threw it at the disgraced pedophile. He stood and walked menacingly toward him. It was time for that five minutes he had wished for! A bailiff stationed at the doors of the courtroom grabbed him. As Solomon cursed and fumed, the bailiff turned him around and escorted him out of the courtroom. Simone and Bethany followed close behind. As he neared the door, Solomon's white clergy collar fell from his pocket to the floor.

7

"But seek first his kingdom and his righteousness, and all these things will be given to you as well."

Matthew 6:33

"Heavenly Father, it's an amazing thing to know You as God *and* Father. I can never thank You enough for welcoming me to be a part of Your family. I can never thank You enough for including me in Your master plan. I can never thank You enough, Lord Jesus, for giving Your perfect life for me. I can never thank You enough, Holy Spirit, for guiding me through this corrupt world. I surrender my all to You, Lord. I trust Your will for my life, Father, so I lay it at Your feet, humbly and completely, submitting to Your direction. You lead, I follow. Lord, in the name of Jesus, I ask that You please forgive me of my sins. Please cleanse me from all unrighteousness. Please fill me with Your Holy Spirit so that the Light of Your Son can shine through me, brighter and brighter. Set me on that hill, Lord so that those who don't know You can see You in me, feel You through me, and be drawn to Your Light in me.

"Lord, please save Mr. Stevenson. Help him fall to his knees and repent before it's too late. Let the world see that You are both just and merciful by restoring a righteous spirit within him and using him, even in jail, to change lives for your glory. Father God, please forgive my daddy. Please extend your grace to him. Please send your angels down and help him. Please help him overcome whatever it is that has pulled him away from You and return to You like never before. For Your glory, Lord. Amen."

Simone stood to her feet and looked at Solomon's incomplete suit of armor hanging on the rack in the corner, his collar probably in a trash heap somewhere. Solomon replaced his minister's uniform with the blue overalls of the plastics factory on the other side of the city, a job he was able to quickly land thanks to a fellow congregant and parent of one of his former students, Sister Janet. It had been a year since Simone saw her daddy suit up for spiritual battle. In fact, it had been a year since she saw Solomon in The Lord's Room at all. It was as if the shackles that fell from her had ensnared him. The spiritual fire that burned white hot in her soul somehow seemed to have used up all of the heavenly fuel, leaving Solomon with dim, smoldering embers. She turned to leave The Lord's Room and wondered if her daddy would ever pick up his cross again.

A year ago, Simone was a budding flower, announcing to the world her voice and her power were here to stay. Today, she is a high school senior tour de force! With Bethany off to college, Simone spread her wings far and wide for all to see. She was a hurdling savant who had a legitimate chance to win the state championship. She was a nearly straight-A student. *Who gets an A in AP chemistry anyway?,* she told herself. She was the best speaker on the debate team. And she had such a humble and gentle personality that even envious teenage girls found it difficult to make up a good reason to hate her, except that all the boys wished they had a chance to go out with her. But Solomon had lowered the shutters, shut the door and locked the gate on their testosterone-driven hopes.

Solomon had always been protective, but that day at the track ratcheted his guardian instincts up a thousand percent. He forced Bethany to break up with her boyfriend at the time and forbade her from seeing anyone until she got to college. Then he lobbied hard to convince her to go to Chadwick State just three miles away. When UCLA offered her a scholarship to its Performing Arts School, she thanked God (for more reasons than one) and packed her bags quickly.

Simone was also under a strict no-boys policy, but she didn't have the same difficulty accepting it. She understood that this stage of her life was meant for more than just adolescent romance. This was her time to feed her relationship with the Lord, to grow in understanding Him and His purpose for her. If she didn't get *that* relationship on Rock-solid footing, it wouldn't matter what other relationship she would try to forge—she knew it wouldn't work anyway. Solomon had Sherrie Walker to thank for helping his little girl come to this precocious understanding.

A few months after the sentencing, Simone had called Sherrie to dish about the best night of her young life. Two of the few events for which Solomon relaxed his stringent no-dating policy were the school proms. Travis Kensley, the fastest sprinter on the team and the best wide receiver in the county, asked Simone to her Junior Prom. Only months removed from the incident, Simone didn't think Solomon would let her go. It would be not only her Junior Prom, it would be her first date! Her jaw dropped to the floor when Solomon said yes.

Solomon knew nothing about makeup, hair or the right gown. Grammy, bless her heart, was a little behind the times, so Simone had to lean on Sherrie. They spent weekend after weekend sifting through catalogs and searching stores until they found the perfect gown, one that accented Simone's beauty as well as her chastity. Sherrie took Simone to the makeup counter at the department store to find the perfect makeup for her beautiful skin. She even combed through magazines to help her find the perfect hairdo. Solomon wasn't a total waste. He would throw on some music in the evenings and (try to) dance with his daughter, and, of course, he paid for all that perfection Sherrie introduced his little girl to.

The night before the big event, Solomon sat his nervous little girl down and said, "Honey, you don't have a thing to be nervous about. This guy,"—he never seemed to remember Travis's name —"is really lucky to be going out with you. You are such a special young lady. It's your night, and it's his job to make you feel like a princess, because that's what you are."

"Thank you, Daddy. Do I still have to bring this?" Simone pulled out the four-ounce bottle of pepper spray Solomon had bought her, the "perfect" first-date gift, in his opinion.

"It's either me or the pepper spray, but one of us is never leaving your side tonight. I'm sure you won't have to use it. I am not worried at all, but you should always be prepared for anything." Solomon was lying. He was more nervous than Simone. He just didn't want to ruin her special night, so he feigned serenity that night and resolved to go the extra mile to ensure his daughter's safety the next night.

Travis arrived in a sweet Ford Mustang his parents rented for the occasion. As he stepped out of the car, his lean six-foot frame and muscled sprinter's shoulders filled out his slim-fitting burgundy tuxedo rather nicely. Solomon watched his every step from the window, examining him for even the slightest hint of malicious intent. As Travis rang the doorbell, Solomon sat.

DING DONG. Still no movement.

DING DONG. Finally, Grammy walked over to the door, glaring at her still-seated son.

"How you doin', young man?"

"Hi, ma'am. My name is Travis. I'm here to pick up Simone."

Solomon studied every word. *So far, so good.*

"Come on in. She'll be right down. This is her father, Mr. Trudeau."

"Hello, sir. My name is Travis. Nice to meet you, Mr. Trudeau."

Solomon locked eyes with the boy, stood up slowly, and extended his hand to accept Travis's invitation to shake. The young suitor didn't seem nearly as comfortable as he did when he stepped out of the car. Solomon squeezed his hand a little harder and a little longer than normal.

Firm handshake. Good eye contact. He might not be that bad.

"Nice to meet you, young man. Please have a seat. So, what are your plans for this evening?"

"Um, I'm taking Simone to the prom, sir."

"Oh. Simone asked for a 2:00 a.m. curfew. The prom's over at midnight, so you should be able to get her back by 12:30, right?"

"Uh, well, sir, a few of us were probably gonna go down to the pier afterward for a little bit."

"Oh, so you do have more planned than just the prom. Were you lying to me, or did you just forget?"

"Uh, no, sir. I wasn't lying, sir. I . . . I just didn't, uh, understand what you me—"

"Why the pier?" Solomon interrupted. "Who's included in this group you're talking about?"

"Uh, some other folks from the track team. We were gonna take pictures at the old lighthouse and have some des—"

"You still haven't told me who's in this 'group.' "

"Sir, there's Brian Lopez and Christie Boyer, uh—"

"Daddy! Leave him alone, please. You know I told you all this already," Simone interrupted, saving poor, young Travis.

"I know, honey. I just want to make sure his story synced up with yours. You kids have fun. Two a.m. Not one second later, Travis. Do you understand?"

"Yes, sir."

Unbeknownst to Simone and Travis, Solomon followed her the entire evening. While Sherrie and Simone prepared for her special evening, Solomon had made some preparations of his own. He had gone to the Salvation Army and bought some clothes Simone would never expect him to wear and then borrowed an old car from their neighbor. As Travis escorted Solomon's princess to his car, Solomon slipped out the back, hopped the gate and sprinted to the borrowed car, which he had parked seven houses down. He followed them to the prom and waited patiently in the car as they danced and laughed their night away. He used his family app to keep track of her movements inside the hall to ensure he knew when they were leaving.

After the prom, he followed her to the pier as well, leaving the car to follow on foot. He saw Travis reach out to hold Simone's hand. It would have been such a tender, sweet moment except for one thing—that was his little girl! He ducked around corners, hid between buildings and even crouched behind a garbage bin, all to ensure his surveillance went undetected. He couldn't ruin this night for her, but he could not leave his little girl alone again— never again. As their evening ended, he realized that he was too exposed to get back to the car without being detected, so he curled up behind the trash can and pretended to be asleep—his empty coffee cup resting beside him. Simone saw the figure lying on the ground. "Oh, how sad. I didn't see him here when we walked up." She opened her purse and put two dollars into the homeless man's cup. *My little girl,* Solomon thought, proudly.

The next morning, Simone called Sherrie to dish about her absolutely fabulous evening! She told her how they danced, and laughed, and talked, and held hands. She even told her how Travis leaned close to her at the pier and said, "You have got to be the most amazing girl I've ever met. I wish this night wouldn't end," and then he kissed her gently on the lips. It was so precious, so priceless. It was the *perfect* first kiss!

Sherrie had heard this before. Sherrie had seen this before. And Sherrie knew she had to instill Godly wisdom before starry-eyed infatuation led another innocent down the path toward heartbreak. "Simone," Sherrie said, "I wish someone would've told me this fifteen years ago. No matter how cute he is or nice he is or smart he is, he's still just a boy, and you're just a girl. Grow up and grow in Him, and I promise you, the man God has for you will put all these boys to shame, and he'll be waiting for you right where you're supposed to be."

It wasn't what Simone expected or wanted to hear. For the first time, Simone didn't want to talk to or be around Sherrie, at least not for a while. She wanted to enjoy her afterglow, and Sherrie's dose of sage wisdom was killing her high. Two weeks later, at a meet, she overheard Travis telling a girl from another team, "You have got to be the most amazing girl I've ever met!" People in the stands could probably hear the thump that Simone's jaw made when it hit the ground. All she could say was "Wow." She said it loud enough for Travis to hear so he would know his smooth game was up. Her afterglow had now fizzled into something more resembling a radioactive fallout. Thankfully, though, Simone wasn't heartbroken. The words of her spiritual sister, whom she hadn't talked to since that discouraging phone call, came flooding back before bitterness could set in. Simone decided then that her heart would not be a buffet line for hungry boys. She was going to focus on Jesus as the Man of her life, and let Him bring the man of her dreams.

8

"All Scripture is God-breathed and is useful for teaching, rebuking, correcting and training in righteousness, so that the servant of God may be thoroughly equipped for every good work."

2 Timothy 3:16-17

Brother Solomon Trudeau eased into his new favorite seat near the back of TCC. It was two rows from the door, and miles away from his old seat on the dais. He was alone today, because Simone felt a little sick, and Grammy stayed back to tend to her. Even though he stepped aside a year ago, he still found himself in church every Sunday. He felt awkward during those first few Sundays after he left the clergy. He imagined daggers thrown from every glance in his direction. Every side conversation in the foyer must have been about the Sunday school teacher who let go of the plow! Every warm hug and handshake were probably masking a cold resentment toward the man who abandoned God and their kids! But he just kept coming—and moving his seat farther and farther back, closer and closer to the door.

Thankfully, those daggers were only sharpened by his

imagination and hurled by his own shame. There probably was a side conversation or two about the former preacher, but it wasn't idle gossip. His church family was praying for him. Pastor Jefferson never disparaged him, never belittled him. Sister Strickland, in particular, was always there to greet him with one of her warm hugs and an encouraging word. Brother Cranston was always there to shake his hand and poke fun at the latest implosion by Solomon's favorite football team—his beloved Browns. Solomon knew their love and concern was genuine, and that realization stopped him from moving his seat all the way out of the congregation.

He wanted to be the old Solomon: the guy who never saw the glass half-empty, the guy who always felt God's presence. These days, a melancholy veil shrouded his heart and mind at all times. He no longer felt God's presence. The glass was still half-full, but he no longer felt joy in the hope that the glass would someday overflow. In church, he was cordial, he stood when the choir sang, he brought his Bible and followed along with the pastor's message, but the veil never lifted. Solomon hoped that if he just kept coming, God would lift that veil and return to him.

Deacon Bradley stepped to the podium and greeted the congregation: "Good morning, TCC."

In unison, the church replied, "Good morning," and then began to clap and cheer as if someone just scored a touchdown.

"This is the day the Lord has made, so let us rejoice and be glad in it!"

The congregation repeated after the deacon: "This is the day the Lord has made, so let us rejoice and be glad in it."

"Please rise and let us lift our voices in reverent worship of our

Lord and Savior, Jesus Christ."

Amazing Grace, how sweet the sound
That saved a wretch like me.

Solomon began singing the familiar hymn with the congregation but then fell silent. He couldn't believe what he was hearing. In the sanctuary full of saints singing, with the deep baritone of Deacon Bradley resonating through the speakers, he could make out a single voice that was so amazingly beautiful, he fell silent to hear it more clearly.

I once was lost, but now am found
Was blind, but now I see.

'Twas grace that taught my heart to fear,
And grace, my fears relieved.
How precious did that grace appear
The hour I first believed.

Through many dangers, toils and snares
I have already come.
T'is grace that brought me safe thus far
And grace will lead me home.

As the hymn finished and the praise and worship team kicked service into high gear, Solomon glanced over his shoulder to see who had this voice of an angel. Sitting across the aisle in the last row was a woman Solomon had never seen before. She sat legs crossed, revealing very tasteful burgundy boots. Long braids flowed from under her stylish gray fedora, which was cocked ever so slightly to the side. Her cashmere turtleneck and leather-trimmed skirt completed a rather striking image. Solomon smiled politely. The stranger smiled and nodded and then returned her focus to the service. He turned his head and tried to focus on the service as well, but his mind kept returning to the hypnotic voice and striking presence of the stranger one row back. There was something about her that he couldn't shake. The last time a voice that wonderful belonged to a woman that striking, Solomon had married her.

After five minutes of announcements, which always felt more like fifty minutes, Deacon Bradley instructed everyone to "please, take some time to fellowship with one another."

Solomon couldn't wait for this part of the service. He fought the urge to rush over to the mystery woman with the voice of an angel, so he slowly stood and greeted the congregants closest to him. *Two or three, then I can make my way across the aisle without looking too anxious.* As he intentionally kept his back toward the stranger, Solomon felt a gentle touch on his shoulder. He turned and beheld the disarming smile of the siren from across the aisle.

"God bless you," she said, as she extended her hand toward Solomon.

"Hello and God bless you. Welcome to TCC. My name is Solomon."

"Hello, I am Gabriella, but everyone calls me Gabby. Nice to meet you."

"I must say, it's been a long time since I have heard such a beautiful singing voice. You truly have a gift."

"Thank you, Solomon." Gabby smiled confidently. Her eye contact was constant, almost piercing. She turned and continued to greet other congregants. Solomon did as well, but he couldn't shake the feeling that this siren had just peered deep into his very soul.

As the service progressed, Pastor Jefferson stepped to the podium to begin his sermon: "Please rise as we read the Word of God, from the Book of Job, Chapter 1, Verses 8 to 12:

Then the LORD said to Satan, 'Have you considered my servant Job? There is no one on earth like him; he is blameless and upright, a man who fears God and shuns evil.'

'Does Job fear God for nothing?' Satan replied. 'Have you not put a hedge around him and his household and everything he has? You have blessed the work of his hands, so that his flocks and herds are spread throughout the land. But now stretch out your hand and strike everything he has, and he will surely curse you to your face.' The LORD said to Satan, 'Very well, then, everything he has is in your power, but on the man, himself do not lay a finger.'"

"You may take your seats."

Everyone sat down, except Solomon. The melancholy veil had lifted to reveal a seething resentment. Solomon couldn't bring himself to sit down because he couldn't stomach the message. He couldn't stomach a spiritual rationalization on how God is so sovereign He can ordain bad things to happen to good people. *Satan did it, but God instigated it, just like with me,* he thought. He couldn't sit, because the wrath he longed to exact against Tim Stevenson locked his knees. He couldn't sit, because the anger over seeing his wife suffer and die compelled him to step into the aisle. He couldn't sit, because the buried burden from a war a decade ago pulled him out the sanctuary and into his car. Solomon started the engine and headed home.

It wasn't the first time Solomon left service early. There was that time, about three weeks after the sentencing, when Pastor Jefferson preached on the very same scripture Sister Strickland had given Solomon. It tasted just as bitter the second time around, so Solomon slipped out twenty minutes into Pastor's sermon. Or that time a few months later, when the announcements were replaced by a testimony period. Solomon skipped out after hearing two known tares praise God for their miraculous healings. But this time was different, and he knew it. This was the first time that the very Word of God pushed him away. No expository words. No dubious testimony. Just scripture. Solomon was overcome with shame. "What the hell's wrong with you?" he shouted as he continued down the road. Despite the storm of emotions churning within him, he couldn't bring himself to turn around. And with each mile, the weight of self-reproach grew heavier, but, still, he couldn't turn around.

POP! The sound of his exploding tire and the jerk of the wheel brought his mind back from the precipitous slopes down which it had started to descend. Solomon gripped the wheel tightly to maintain control of the car and guided it safely to the side of the road. "That figures," he mumbled, as he put the car in park and exited to survey the damage. *You gotta be kiddin' me!* Solomon put both hands on his hips and just shook his head. Both passenger-side tires had blown out! Nobody has two spares. Solomon hopped on the phone to see if Grammy could drive out to meet him, but the phone went to voicemail. *Come on, Mama. How many times do I have to tell her to turn her phone on?* Next he tried Simone, but hers just rang and rang, and he couldn't leave a message because the voicemail was full. Solomon looked up and let out an exasperated sigh. *Really? Well, might as well get one changed before trying them again.* He removed his jacket, rolled up his sleeves and got to work.

As Solomon tightened the lug nuts on the spare, he heard a car pull to a stop in front of his. He looked up but didn't recognize it. *Clop, Clop, Clop.* The driver's hard-soled shoes announced her advance. As she rounded the front of his car, he looked up to his right and spied a familiar pair of alluring burgundy boots. It was the siren!

"Looks like somebody's not having a good day. Who gets two flat tires?"

"Not just flats—blowouts! You know what they say, 'Go big or go home,' " Solomon replied. It was the first time he had felt any amount of happiness that day.

"Who was the last one to put air in your tires?"

"I'd love to blame somebody else, but then I'd probably blow the other two tires out 'cause of karma."

Gabby laughed. "Do you need me to call somebody?"

"Well, I was gonna try my mother and daughter after I fixed this one."

"How far away are they?"

"Not sure. My house is another fifteen minutes up the road, but they didn't answer, so I don't know if they're even there."

"Tell you what. I'll let you borrow my spare so you can get home."

"Really? That is so nice of you. Thank you so much."

"I can't just leave you on the side of the road when I know I have the means to help you. Besides, I'm pretty sure I can track you down before you skip town with my tire." They both laughed. As Solomon tightened the last nut on the first tire, Gabby opened her trunk and moved some bags to the side. "I'll let you get it out. I'm not exactly dressed for manual labor today."

"No," said Solomon, rising and walking toward her trunk. "You're dressed a whole lot better than that."

Solomon smiled but felt like smacking himself upside the head. *That's the best comeback you can muster, Solly?* Solomon was never the silver-tongued, debonair type. He never needed to be—until now. *Ugh, I suck at this*, he admitted to himself.

"Thank you, Solomon."

Crap! She remembered my name? Solomon just smiled as he reached down to extract her spare, desperately racking his brain, hoping to remember her name. *What was it—Bella, Daniella, Greta . . .*

"You know, you can just ask me for my name again," she said.

Solomon's smile faded. He was completely blowing it! "I'm sorry. I am just terrible with names. What—"

"Gabby," she interrupted. "How long have you been attending that church?"

"Over ten years. Was today your first visit? I don't recall seeing you before."

"I have stopped by a few times. I live about thirty minutes away, but I enjoy the service, so I stop in when I can. Pastor's message was pretty powerful. What did you think?"

Huh, Solomon thought, *how could she not see me walk out? I walked right past her down the center aisle.*

"It's a great sermon. He's preached on that scripture in the past. It's always very enlightening, very edifying."

"So true. The Book of Job is just overflowing with nuggets of wisdom and revelation. It's one of my favorite books of the Bible. What part of the message resonated with you?"

You gotta be kiddin' me, lady. I left early for a reason, so I don't want to think about the nuggets I left behind! "Actually, I left early. I had to be somewhere. Then this happened, so I missed out for nothing."

"Well, after reading the scripture, the pastor told a really amazing story about how he had his own Job experience years ago, before he became a pastor. He said he had just gotten baptized when all hell broke loose in his life. He said he lost his home, his job, his dad and his fiancé within three years. Then he told us all something I don't think anyone knew—his fiancé left him after they had a miscarriage! I was blown away. He was so transparent, so vulnerable. I had never heard a pastor admit to fornication, a child out of wedlock and major tribulation—in the same sermon!" Neither had Solomon. He suddenly felt deep empathy for his pastor, who had revealed something so personal, and in some respect, so shameful, to the whole congregation.

"Then he talked about how God was sovereign and can do whatever he wants to whomever he wants."

Here we go. Now I remember why I left.

"Then he said something I'll never forget: 'God doesn't allow trials, loss and pain on a whim, nor does he do it for sadistic amusement. He allows misfortune to come upon His chosen so that we can grow, so that we can prosper in Him, and so that He can get the maximum glory from our lives.' Pastor said we can't always blame God. Sometimes He ordains it, but sometimes we choose it and He just lets us wallow in the mess we created. Either way, the only thing God can't do is lie, and He said, 'All things work together for good to them that love Him and are the called according to His purpose.' So, if we trust Him and trust *in* Him, and persevere 'til the end, we'll look back and see God carried us through it all and placed us on higher ground when all is said and done."

"Wow, that was pretty powerful," Solomon said, sincerely. The Cliff's Notes version that Gabby relayed struck a chord in him as well. "Thank you, Gabby. I'll be chewing on that for a while. And thanks for the tire. All done!"

"Wonderful. I would like to pray for you before we go." She reached out her hand. Solomon placed his hand in hers as she closed her eyes and lowered her head. "God of all creation, Lord of the heavenly host, our great Father, thank You for this divine appointment. There's no such thing as coincidences, only God-incidences. Thank you for sending me by just when my brother in Christ needed me. Thank you for delivering your message to an open heart who almost missed it, but in your providence, you made a way—even at the cost of two tires. Please watch over Solomon. Please help him get home safely. In Jesus' name, Amen. OK. You take care, Solomon."

"Wait, how do I reach you to return your spare?" Solomon asked.

"I'll find you. I know where you'll be next Sunday, right?" She smiled, playfully.

"Yes, you do. 'Til then, Gabby."

"God bless you, Solomon."

9

"Refrain from anger and turn from wrath; do not fret—it leads only to evil."

Solomon was giddy. It was a rare sight these days to see him so happy. If the Browns won, he'd be bouncing around the house dapping Simone and high-fiving Grammy the rest of the day. If he heard one of Gloria's favorite songs on the radio, he'd smile from ear to ear and allow his mind to drift through warm memories of his love-struck youth. But the veil always descended within a few hours to a day. This time was different. Solomon had been happy for a few days, his mood almost jolly. Maybe it was the stranger with the voice of an angel who showed up out of nowhere to save the day. She definitely occupied more of his thoughts than any woman had in quite some time. He was intrigued and looked forward to Sunday to see what the next page in this new drama had in store. But intrigue does not equal jolly. No, this mood found its genesis in another source. Another woman had reappeared!

His oldest daughter called that Monday and surprised the Trudeaus with news of an unexpected visit! Bethany's college roommate had access to airline buddy passes, courtesy of her ticket-agent mother, and was happy to share them with her roomie. She decided to fly home this coming weekend for an unplanned "brain-break" as she called it. The unexpected news sent Solomon to giddy-land. He hadn't seen his little girl in months and was excited to have his whole family—well, most of it—back together again. It was perfect timing, too. This coming Friday was opening night for another blockbuster. Solomon and the girls had made a mini-tradition of enjoying opening weekend together—the long lines and crowded theaters didn't feel as long or as crowded because they made it their own family event. They would arrive early enough to get plenty of snacks and find good seats, then sit laughing and chatting away until the previews started. It was a tradition he missed, and one he knew would be ending for good all too soon. So Solomon couldn't wait for the weekend to come!

Standby sucks, Bethany thought, before catching herself. *But nowhere near as much as paying for a ticket.* She was on her third hour in LAX, hoping the next flight would be the one that would take her back home. Airports are such awesome places to people-watch —thousands of people hustling back and forth, some frustrated at the ordeal; others excited by what awaits them at some distant tarmac. There were families anxious to reunite; lovers anxious to embark on a new adventure; corporate titans ready to close the deal. The airport was a smorgasbord of scenarios, offering a creative soul like Bethany endless imaginative possibilities to explore.

That couple over there. They must be on their honeymoon! So young, holding hands as they sit, chatting away. They are probably on their way to Sydney! An Outback adventure awaits them, followed by a close encounter with the Great Barrier Reef.

Over there, that woman with the five-hundred-dollar shoes and fifty-thousand-dollar facelift, she's on her way to some swanky socialite gathering in New York. Dom Perignon and truffles will be passed around the posh soirée, like Red Bull and chips at the dorm.

That one is an enigma. Rugged Levi's. Tag Heuer watch. Duffel bag. With that confident stride and toned physique, he's the real-life Ethan Hunt. He definitely knows more than a few ways to kill a man. And the woman walking with him isn't really "with" him. There is no affection; she walks with equal confidence, equal purpose. They are probably on their way to Moscow, via Budapest. Their top-secret op will make those Russkies pay for messing with our elections.

And so it went, hour after hour. Bethany envisioned scenario after scenario to keep her mind active and unfocused on the tedium of the day. In all her observations and mental postulations, it never occurred to her to strike up a conversation with anyone. She was content to dance away in her own cerebral studio, where she was most comfortable.

Bethany was an introvert at heart, and she was perfectly fine with that. Though she was anxious to move to the metropolis on the coast, she wasn't keen on exploring everything this newfound freedom had to offer. She wanted to see more of life than Solomon had allowed, but she didn't want to partake in all she saw. So that meant going out with friends but ensuring she was back in her dorm, in her right mind, before it got too late. And it meant minding her own business, rather than walking up to complete strangers and actually talking to them.

Around 4:30, Bethany finally made it onto a flight back home. She couldn't wait to sit down, throw on her headphones and zone out. Her brain-break couldn't begin until she knew for sure she was going home. She got a middle seat near the back of the plane, which was to be expected if she got any seat at all.

"Excuse me, that's my seat," she said to the aisle-seat occupant.

Looking somewhat annoyed, the man stood up to let her by. Bethany was caught off guard by his mass—he was immense! His head almost touched the ceiling, and he was about as wide as the entire aisle. He wore a white T-shirt with a black skull-and-crossbones emblem on the front. His beard was thick and unkept. "There you go, miss," he replied and proceeded to hack and cough up some disgusting wad of phlegm that was basking in the dark recesses of his throat.

"Thank you." *I may have to skip the buddy pass next time,* she thought. *Ain't worth it!*

There was a middle-aged man sitting next to the window. He had his earphones on, eyes closed, arms folded and the shade drawn. Bethany couldn't wait to follow his lead. She sat down and immediately pulled out her phone to cue her "Brain-Break" playlist; she had compiled it the day before for the three-hour flight. She plopped her earpieces in, turned the music on and placed her best "Do Not Disturb" look on her face. *Let the brain-break begin!*

As God would have it, Bethany's plan took a detour. Twenty-minutes into the flight, the music stopped. Bethany opened her eyes and inspected her phone, only to discover the battery was so depleted, her phone was automatically shutting down nonessential functions, which included her music.

"You gotta be kidding me," she said. To her dismay, the behemoth on the aisle apparently saw the opening and took it.

"Ran out of juice, eh?" he asked.

Great. Here we go. Now I gotta deal with this guy! He's probably been doing mental gymnastics on my friggin' cup size since I sat down.

"Yeah. Hope I can get to sleep without it." *Please take the hint. Please!*

"Who needs sleep when you got this big ol' teddy bear to talk to?" He laughed and then reached into his pocket and pulled out a small metal block. "Just messin' with ya. I got some readin' to do, so I won't be needin' this. Sweet dreams." He handed her the block, which turned out to be a portable power source.

"Wow. Thank you so much," Bethany replied. As she plugged her phone into the power pack and closed her eyes again, she couldn't seem to find peace this time. The unsolicited kindness of the mammoth seated next to her was a stark contrast to her cold shoulder. She cracked an eye open to see what he was reading. It was the Bible. *Crap, I suck.*

The Trudeaus piled into the car and headed to the theater. Family Movie Night had arrived! Grammy rarely went with them to movie night ("Last time I checked, it's the same movie on DVD, without all the fuss," she would say), but this time she wanted to soak up every moment possible with her grandkids. Solomon let Simone drive them to the theater for the first time, so she was excited and nervous.

"Remember, right is 'go'; left is 'stop,' " Bethany teased.

"Shut up and let me concentrate," Simone snapped back, fully focused on getting them there safely.

"You know, if you go any slower, we'll make it just in time for the closing credits," Bethany quipped.

"You know, I don't remember being such a pain in the butt when Dad let you drive us all for the first time."

"You're right; you weren't. Too late now. You missed your window, li'l sis." Solomon had missed the playful banter between his little girls.

There were a ton of people at the theater. The new release was the latest superhero installment, so a big crowd was expected. When they arrived, the Trudeaus were confronted by a super long line to buy tickets, a bunch of lines at the snack counter and a steadily growing line at the door leading into the theater. Solomon had already bought tickets for him and the girls a few days earlier, but Grammy was a surprise tagalong, so it was time to divide and conquer. Solomon would wait outside to buy one more ticket, Bethany would take everyone's order and wait in the snack line, and Simone would get a place in line at the theater before it got even longer.

Bethany walked Grammy over to a bench near the video games to take a seat and people-watch until the theater opened for seating. "Be right back, Grammy," she said and hurried off to stand in line at the snack counter. *Three large popcorns, one nachos 'n cheese, two packs of Raisinets and four hot dogs, extra relish on one.* Bethany had a lot to remember, so she kept repeating the orders out loud to herself. "Three large popcorns, one nachos 'n cheese, two—"

"You know, you may want to write all that down. By the time you get to the front, who knows what you'll end up ordering." The smooth voice came from behind. She wheeled around irked, ready to give the interrupter a nasty little look and snide response. Her eyes encountered a chest full of thick muscles, enticingly masked by a white turtleneck. Her eyes traveled across the vast plain, from one shoulder to another. Then she tilted up, and up, to see a smile that melted a bit of the ice she had intended to throw his way. When her eyes finally met his, she had to catch herself—the man was gorgeous.

"Didn't think to bring a notepad with me to the movies," Bethany responded, after picking her jaw up off the floor.

"Good point," the Adonis responded, "but I'm pretty sure you did think to bring your phone."

"Duh. Good idea. I didn't even know I was thinking out loud. Thanks."

"Better hurry before you end up buying ten hot dogs, twenty-four boxes of popcorn, eleven Twizzlers—"

"No, stop, stop, stop!" she blurted, covering her ears with both hands. Then she turned around, grabbed her cell and started reciting the order into a text message to Simone. As she finished, the tall, handsome stranger reinstated his skilled, well-practiced approach.

"I'm sorry. Just having a little fun at your expense. My name is Errol." He reached out his hand, holding it patiently, confident that his advance would be reciprocated.

Bethany, spellbound by his entrancing eyes, shook his hand. "Nice to meet you, Errol. I'm Bethany."

"Beautiful."

"What?" Bethany asked.

"Your name. It's beautiful and unique. It suits you, very nicely."

"You think so?"

"I know so."

As he spoke, Bethany stopped looking *at* him and started looking *into* him—into his eyes. Something just wasn't right. Behind those beautiful eyes lay an empty soul. Behind that strong chest lay a heart that was only true to itself. Beneath the sculpture with the disarming smile, Bethany saw a predator on the hunt. All of sudden, the spell lifted.

"Well, thank you. When my father gets here, I'll be sure to let him know how thoughtful you are." Bethany turned back around just in time to place her order.

Errol's weren't the only pair of eyes fixed on Bethany. Grammy saw Errol coming a mile away. She saw him staring at Bethany as she walked away from the video game area. She saw him follow Bethany to the line, rushing to ensure he was right behind her. And she saw him ogling her from behind, waiting for the opportunity to speak to her. She saw Bethany melt when confronted by his beauty and stature. She had seen enough. Grammy closed her eyes and began to pray for her granddaughter. *Lord, please open my baby's eyes and show her what's really there. Cover her, dear God, and shield her right now. In Jesus' name, Amen.*

From outside the theater, Solomon was also able to see the mini-drama unfold. As Errol followed Bethany to the line, Solomon went on red alert. As Errol scanned his little girl up and down, Solomon went to DEFCON 2. That big vein on the side of his head started to pulsate; his hands involuntarily closed into fists; his body leaned forward ready to take down the young hunter if he even looked like he would threaten his little girl. He left the ticket line and walked slowly toward the front doors. Coiled. Ready.

As Bethany collected her order, Errol stepped forward for one more attempt to reel in this prized catch. "Here, let me help you 'til your old man gets here."

Old man? This guy is definitely just a pretty shell at the beach— absolutely nothing inside. "No, thank you, Errol. I'll manage just fine until my 'old man' gets here."

Undaunted, he reached to "help" her with the unstable tower of popcorn. "That's gonna fall any second," he warned.

Bethany stopped. She was getting annoyed, but she didn't want to make a scene and ruin the evening. "Errol, 'no, thank you' means—noooooooo!"

Bethany started the sentence talking to Errol, but finished it pleading to Solomon. Solomon snapped! He ran into the theater, past the ticket agent, and cold-cocked the big, would-be Casanova, sending him sprawling to the floor. Errol smacked his head on the floor and lay there motionless, out cold. Solomon was so enraged he didn't realize he had knocked Bethany over to get to Errol. When he looked down at his little girl on the floor, her eyes alight with fear, Solomon returned to his senses. He dropped to his knees, still looking at his horrified little girl.

"Oh my God, what have I done?"

Solomon sat quietly in disbelief as security hovered over him. There were no tears, but his hands quivered uncontrollably and his head hung low. He was a stew of adrenaline, shame, confusion and remorse, a mix of emotions he hadn't felt since Iraq. Errol came to quickly and was eager to know what had happened. Security had taken him to the manager's office to see if paramedics were necessary and to report the assault. They also wanted to separate the two men to prevent round two from starting. The girls couldn't get near Solomon—security couldn't take the chance of him coming unhinged again—so they stood on the other side of the room with Grammy. Bethany and Simone were in shock, but Grammy had an otherworldly calm about her. She watched the entire affair from the bench and brought the girls over to her when Solomon was still kneeling next to his victim.

The police didn't take long to come. This wasn't the first time they had to respond to what they assumed was an opening-night dustup between a bunch of testosterone-rich boys. How surprised they were when they saw the middle-aged, former minister Solomon Trudeau somberly awaiting their arrival.

"Pastor Solomon?" one officer asked, with a look of utter shock on his face.

Just when Solomon thought he had hit rock bottom, he looked up and tumbled even lower. "Hello, Robbie," Solomon replied dejectedly. Years earlier, Roberto Hernandez had been one of Solomon's students in his Teen Christian Living class.

Officer Hernandez was only four months out of the academy and still in the probationary period. He had worked the jails a bit, did some traffic stops and even served some high-risk warrants, but nothing prepared him for seeing his former mentor broken—the perp he was called to arrest. The searing glare from his pissed-off senior officer helped him snap back into the moment.

"We have a job to do, Officer," the senior officer said, as he waited to see if the rookie could regain his bearings.

"Yes, sir," Officer Hernandez shot back quickly as he pulled his handcuffs out. "Pastor, uh, Mr. Trudeau, you are under arrest for assault and trespassing. You have the right to remain silent. Anything you say can be used against you in a court of law. You have the right to an attorney . . . ”

Solomon thought: *I ran over my oldest daughter, to assault a kid, in front of my mother and youngest daughter, on Family Movie Night, and now I'm being arrested by my Sunday school student. How did I get here?*

Both girls sobbed and held onto Grammy. “Wait here,” Grammy said to her granddaughters as she got up and started to walk across the room toward her prodigal son. The officers were leading him to their car when the senior officer saw the old woman approaching. With a stern, unsympathetic voice, he said, “Ma’am, please stay back. This man is going to jail. There’s nothing we need to discuss.”

“Officer, that man is my son. I’m not trying to stop you; he deserves to go to jail. May I please talk to my son?”

“OK, ma’am. One minute.”

“Won’t take nearly that long, Officer. Solomon, I’m ashamed of the way you acted tonight. That was not the man your daddy and I raised. Remember who you are. You are my son, and I love you. It’s time to get up, son. It's time to get up."

The officers walked Solomon to the police car, and Grammy returned to the girls. “You two ready?”

“Yeah. Let’s go,” Simone replied.

Both girls got up and headed toward the exit, but Grammy walked the other way.

“Grammy, where you going?”

“It’s Family Movie Night. I’m at the movie theater. I got a ticket. Where do you think I’m going?”

“Aren’t we gonna go bail Dad out?” Bethany asked, with a confused look on her face.

“He’s right where he needs to be. When the Lord knocks you

off your feet, sometimes you need to stay on the ground a little while. We'll get him in the morning."

Solomon Trudeau looked out the window from the back of the police car and saw Grammy heading toward the theater as his little girls somberly followed behind. Family Movie Night lived on, without him.

Solomon had never seen a cell, let alone the inside of one, until now. As the bars closed behind him, he looked down at his ink-stained finger in disbelief. "Where did that come from?" he wondered out loud. He'd been mad before; he'd been in fights before; he even shot and killed people in war. But there was only one other time when he tried to physically attack another man with his bare hands. There was only one other time when rage overwhelmed his sensibilities.

It was a year ago, in that courtroom, when Tim Stevenson disrespected his family and mocked his one baby girl by coming on to his other baby girl. *That was different. That was understandable,* he thought. *But this? If that floor hadn't been carpeted, I could have sent that boy to the emergency room. Even though I didn't like him pursuing Bethany, I didn't have to take him down. He was just doing what young men do. What's going on with me?* Solomon knew he would have at least a few hours to ruminate on the absurdity of the evening; the movie was two and a half hours. But as three hours turned into four, he realized his stint behind bars might not end quickly. Grammy was sending her son a message.

10

"Create in me a clean heart, O God, and renew a steadfast spirit within me. Do not cast me away from Your presence, and do not take Your Holy Spirit from me. Restore to me the joy of Your salvation, and uphold me by Your generous Spirit."

Psalm 51:10-12

"Solomon Trudeau," the guard belted out, startling Solomon awake. He had not gotten to sleep until deep into the night, and the guard rattled the cell open around 7:30 a.m. "You made bail."

Solomon shook the cobwebs loose and quietly walked out of the cell, still in a state of disbelief over his actions the previous night. As the officer led him through the release procedures, shame started to overwhelm him. *What do I say to my girls? What do I say to Mama?* Solomon felt he had shrunk a few feet overnight. How could his little girls look up to him after last night? How could they respect him after seeing him devolve into an anger-possessed ruffian? Solomon didn't know the answer but girded up his loins, because he would soon find out. As he pushed open the door that led to the lobby, he looked all around but didn't see his family. As he panned the faces, he backtracked to one he recognized—Gabby. Astonishment replaced his sullen expression.

"Gabby? What are you doing here?"

"Hello, Solomon. I'm the one who bailed you out."

"Oh! Th-th-thank you," Solomon stammered hard, trying to get the words out. The last person he expected to see was the woman who came to his rescue a week ago. And here she was again to save the day.

"I was at the movie theater last night and saw them putting you into the police car. I made a couple of calls and found out that you were still here, so I decided to come down and help you out. I won't regret it, right?"

"No, ma'am. Thank you. Uh, I'm sorry you had to see me like this."

"I've seen worse, Solomon. You're probably hungry; I am too. Let's go get something to eat. You're buying."

"This is the second time you've saved me. Breakfast is the least I can do," Solomon replied.

As Gabby drove them to a diner a few blocks away, Solomon was pleasantly surprised and thoroughly relieved that she didn't bring up the jail, the arrest and, most of all, the offense. They just chit-chatted about normal stuff—the weather, the Browns, the clunking noise they heard under the car—anything and everything but Solomon's brief incarceration. Solomon started to forget about the cellar he had just sunk into; it almost felt like a date. But that changed at the restaurant as soon as they both placed their orders.

"So," Gabby transitioned, as she handed the menu to the waiter, "what happened to you Solomon?" Her inquisitive yet concerned tone left no doubt what she was referring to. Solomon came crashing back to reality.

"Uh, well, last night I kinda lost my head," Solomon answered, hoping he could slide through this awkward, embarrassing topic with as few details as possible.

"Oh, I know what happened last night, Solomon."

She already knows? Solomon thought.

"I know that you attacked a horny young man for nothing."

Nothing! Solomon started to feel the anger well up within him. His jaw tightened and his eyes furrowed. "Look, I shouldn't have decked the guy, but it wasn't 'nothing.' "

Gabriella's expression never changed, and her peace never left her, even though Solomon was obviously agitated. She continued: "A young man had the audacity to come on to a beautiful young lady. As a father, you should protect your daughter; that is honorable. But what isn't honorable is attacking someone without at least giving them the opportunity to explain themselves, or apologize for how they may have wronged you. What isn't honorable is allowing anger to become wrath. You're an honorable man, Solomon. So, I'm asking you, what happened?"

Her eyes didn't leave his. She didn't even blink. Solomon understood what she meant. *She's not asking what happened last night; she's asking what happened to me!* Solomon paused. The question pricked his heart, because it went deeper than he was prepared to go. He had asked himself the same question more than once, but this is the first time he felt truly convicted to search himself for the answer. Solomon sat silently for a long time, pondering the question. A part of him hoped the pregnant pause would make Gabby uncomfortable enough to change the subject and let him off the hook, but her focus never wavered.

Solomon dropped his head, cleared his throat and said, "Let's just say I fell into a hole about a year ago, and I . . . hmm, I haven't been able to climb out yet."

"We don't usually fall when we're just standing still. So, you must have been walking a path. What was that path?"

What? This lady keeps knocking on doors I don't want to open. I'm done! But the deeply concerned look in Gabby's eyes completely disarmed Solomon's defiant bravado. As much as he wanted to get up and walk right out the front door—and all the way home if he had too—he felt compelled to answer. It was as if his body were scratching and clawing to leave but couldn't muster the strength to extricate itself from the chair or disengage from Gabby's purposeful stare.

"Well, I used to be a youth pastor," Solomon finally answered.

"And now, you're not?"

"Now, I'm not."

Gabby leaned back as the waiter placed her food in front of her. "Thank you," she said to her server.

Solomon was relieved to see the pancakes and bacon set before him. In truth, it could have been a plate of cardboard and sawdust as long as it saved him from having to go farther down memory lane.

"Perfect timing," he said. "We're starving!"

"Will you bless the meal?" Gabby asked.

"Sure. Lord, thank you for this food. Please bless it and the hands that prepared it. Amen."

"Amen."

Solomon decided to lighten the mood and change the subject. "You know, you're making me look pretty bad. Your fruit, wheat toast and jam are a helluva lot healthier than my pancakes, bacon and butter."

Gabby gave a polite smile and replied, "Well, you didn't see the hot dog, soda and nachos I had last night."

They both laughed, and, for a moment, Solomon thought he had escaped, but his hopes flickered away in an instant.

"When I first saw you last Sunday in service," Gabby reengaged, "I felt a deep, heavy melancholy surrounding you. You sang the songs, you prayed the prayers, but you never felt the joy of the Lord. It was as if your body was in the building, but your heart was still at the door, wondering whether to stay or go. Stepping down from the pulpit, that's a pretty steep fall, but I don't believe your spiritual crisis began the day you put your collar down. That was just the day it came out of the closet for all to see. It was the day you stopped pretending. So, Solomon, what . . . happened?"

Now Solomon knew there was no escape. Though he wanted to shut it down or run away, he just couldn't. All of a sudden, Solomon found himself struggling to hold back tears. As he fumbled around for an answer, he realized he hadn't talked about that day in the courtroom, or the assault that precipitated it, since it all had happened. Pastor Jefferson had tried multiple times to meet with him following his resignation, but he always found a way to disappear into the exiting congregation, or just blatantly ignore his call. Grammy tried to talk to him about it, but he would change the subject or kiss her on the forehead and leave the room. Bethany would text him every now and then to ask, "Did you find your collar yet?" but he never took the bait. The only person who hadn't tried was Simone. She just replaced him in The Lord's Room, privately praying for her prodigal daddy.

Solomon knew deep down that he couldn't lock it away anymore. This was not something he could shut down or walk away from. After a long pause, he cleared his throat, wiped away the single tear that had escaped and trickled down his cheek, and then began to peel back the bandage he had placed over his festering spiritual wound.

"My daughter, Simone . . . there was this coach that I trusted. He was her private track coach. Former Olympian. Really top-shelf, everybody thought. He recognized her talent and agreed to coach her for free. I thought he was a true gift from God. One day, I left my little girl—" Solomon's voice broke. There's no stopping the tears now. He struggled to speak but the boulder in his throat just kept getting bigger and bigger. Gabby reached across the table to grab his hand and gently squeezed it as if to say, "You're not alone; you can do this."

Solomon felt the comforting gesture chip away at that boulder, so he cleared his throat, drank a little orange juice and continued: "One day I left my little girl with him at the track, and he assaulted her. She was strong enough to fight him off before he could . . . before it got worse. After they arrested him, we found out Simone wasn't the only one. There were many, many others. He was a predator and had been doing that for years. The previous victims kept quiet because they idolized him, and he held their dreams in his hands. He was convicted, but he wasn't sorry. Matter of fact, at the sentencing, that . . . that as- . . . that guy had the audacity to smile at Simone and wink at Bethany! I lost it and just rushed the guy. If I would have made it, I'd be the one in prison—and he'd be dead."

"God help us," Gabby said as she squeezed Solomon's hand.

"That must have been so horrible for you and your family. There is so much evil in this world. Sometimes I wonder how any Light at all can shine in this darkness. I think any dad worth his salt would want to ring that guy's neck. Your anger was justified . . . is justified. But wrath never is, Solomon. What that man tried to do to Simone—what he did do to so many others—is almost unforgivable."

Almost! The word hung in the air like a putrid stench. Solomon looked at Gabby with so much venom that she let his hand go and leaned back. She sensed her words had opened the door to a deep darkness in a man just a few feet away.

"What did you say? How dare you! How would you feel if some pervert attacked your child?! Tried to steal her innocence?! Oh wait, you don't have a clue what this feels like, 'cause you don't have any kids! So don't you dare sit there and tell me that son of a bitch is forgivable! He's right where he belongs, and all he deserves is the feeling of my boot on his ass!"

The foul language that came rushing out shocked Solomon as much as it did Gabby. He hadn't cursed like that since his days in the military. "I'm sorry, I don't know where that came from. I apologize for speaking to you that way, but you hit a nerve, obviously."

"Solomon, I know exactly where those words came from. They came from a place so filled with pain and wrath, that you struggle to keep the venom in. A place so clouded by guilt that you can't seem to find your way anymore. A place so steeped in confusion that you can't tell who you're truly angry with. Those words came from your heart, Solomon. Your heart. That man deserves to be where he is, but you do not. You're both in prison."

There was a long silence. Gabby had a way of issuing rebuke that abounded in love, then letting Solomon silently marinate in the admonition. Instantly, scripture kept coming forth from the recesses of his mind: "Out of the abundance of the heart, the mouth speaks." "Be angry, and do not sin; do not let the sun go down on your wrath." "Not returning evil for evil or reviling for reviling, but on the contrary blessing, knowing that you were called to this, that you may inherit a blessing."

It was as if a floodgate of God's word had been opened, a gate Solomon had closed over a year ago. He sat in silence, awash in a torrent of Word buffeting the darkness that had overtaken his heart.

After nearly a minute had passed, Gabby asked, "How is Simone?"

Solomon looked up, and for the first time in what felt like forever, he smiled. "Simone is awesome. Immediately after the assault, she was an emotional wreck, of course, but by the time the sentencing came, she morphed into Wonder Woman. She isn't walking around scared. She isn't angry at the world. At anyone, as far as I can tell. Not even Stevenson. She says she forgave him at the sentencing! She's praying and reading the Bible more than ever before. She talks about that day without any tears—no fear, no self-doubt, no shame. Somehow, that mountain became a molehill for her. I truly thank God for that."

Gabby took notice. It was the first time she had heard Solomon mention God. "Praise the Lord. God will do some amazing things through her. Isn't it interesting how one horrible act can send two people in totally opposite directions? One grew stronger in the Lord; the other stumbled back from Him. One is soaring; the other still can't seem to find his footing. Simone embraced her Father, while your anger made you leave your cross on the floor."

On the floor. How did she know? Solomon thought. But before he could speak, Gabby continued.

"Your daughter is free, Solomon. But you're still bound in chains—chains that were probably forged long before Tim Stevenson showed up."

With that last blow, Solomon crumbled. The conversation careened even deeper into his secret place. That dark corner where Solomon had stored the pain, anger and despair forged from a life lived in the trenches—a life in which he failed to protect his family from a predator; a life in which the prayers he lifted for his ailing wife were unanswered; a life in which he saw the absolute worst in men, and himself, on a battlefield thousands of miles away. Solomon lowered his head into his hands and began to sob. It didn't matter that he was crying like a baby in front of a woman, or that the people at the other tables were looking at him, or that the waiter had brought their food. Gabby had cracked a chamber so full of tears, nothing could stop them from falling. Gabby slid next to Solomon and gently held him as the torrent continued. She motioned to the stunned waiter and mouthed silently, "We'll take this to go."

"Hurry up!" Simone yelled. She had grown accustomed to pretty much having her own bathroom since Bethany left for college. Grammy used Solomon's bathroom most of the time.

"Patience is a virtue, little sister," Bethany replied from the other side of the door.

"You can't even spell virtue! Hurry up!"

"And for that, I think I'll paint my toes. Different colors. Left-handed. This is precise work, so I might be a while."

"Ugh! Some days I really love you, and some days I can't stand you. Guess what today is!" Simone stormed off to Solomon's bathroom. His always seemed so—yucky. Using a boy's bathroom was bad enough, but using your dad's bathroom—sitting on the same toilet he sits on; seeing the randomly placed, twice-used underwear strewn ever so grotesquely on the same towel he used to dry his wrinkling hide, then trying to find her reflection in a mirror caked with a month's worth of toothpaste remnants—it was just more than Simone could bear this early in the morning. But nature called. Actually, nature was screaming at the top of her lungs, and Bethany left her no choice. "Ugh, will he ever put the toilet seat down?!"

Grammy was already downstairs. There was no time for a nice Saturday breakfast; her son had spent enough time behind bars. Last night she was content to let him cool his heels and ruminate on his present condition, but this morning, her motherly instincts were in high gear. She needed to get her son out of that place and bring him home.

"Come on, girls! We gotta get going. Your father's been there long enough."

Simone heard the fervency in the voice of her normally soft-spoken grandmother, but this was a process that couldn't be rushed. "Coming!" she replied.

After a few minutes, Simone came running down the stairs. Grammy and Bethany were both in the kitchen enjoying some juice. When Simone arrived, Grammy set her glass down and took both girls by the hand.

"Girls," Grammy began, "I need you to listen to me now. Your father is a good man, who made a terrible mistake last night. I raised him right, so I know he is very ashamed, especially that he acted like that in front of you. He is your daddy, and you will honor him. God is not even close to being through with him yet. When you see him, you don't have to act like nothing happened, but you better act like his little girls. He's going through a serious battle, and neither one of you is grown enough to counsel him, belittle him, berate him or disrespect him. Love him, pray for him, period. You understand?"

"Yes, Grammy," both girls replied in unison.

"Alright. Let's pray. Dear Lord, we thank you for your many blessings and amazing grace. Lord, we ask your forgiveness for our sins, for they are ever before us. Father God, please forgive my boy. You know his heart. You know the pain that's darkening his world. We stand on your word, 'cause we know all things work together for good for them that love you and are called according to your purpose. We stand on your word that tells us you are like a refiner's fire. Lord, please see Solomon through this season and bring him out on the other side restored as pure gold. For your glory and name's sake. Amen."

Grammy reached out and hugged each girl, and they headed for the front door. Bethany grabbed Simone's hand. They looked at each other and just smiled. No matter how much they couldn't stand each other on a given day, they always loved each other every day.

Grammy opened the front door and stepped onto the porch and stopped in her tracks. Solomon was shuffling up the walkway. His eyes were glazed and bloodshot, his shoulders forward, his countenance sullen. In that instant, Grammy didn't see a grown man; she saw her baby boy, emotionally battered and bruised. Grammy couldn't hold back any longer. She rushed to her little boy and hugged him tight as tears rolled down her cheeks. The girls followed close behind. Simone noticed a car she hadn't seen before driving away. They all just hugged Solomon silently, each one trying to magically infuse him with their own energy, mystically tape him back together with their own affection, spiritually straighten him up with their love. And Solomon needed every ounce of it!

"Let's go inside, baby." Grammy finally broke the silent embrace. There was no talk of last night, or the jail. Not today. One look from Grammy let the girls know that the subject was off-limits—for now.

11

"The Lord is righteous in all his ways and faithful in all he does. The Lord is near to all who call on him, to all who call on him in truth. He fulfills the desire of those who fear him; he also hears their cry and saves them."

Matthew 4:4

Solomon spent the whole day in his bedroom, deep in thought. He had brought the leftovers home with him but didn't touch it. The turmoil within erased any desire to eat. He tried sitting at the window, sitting on the edge of the bed, and lying down and staring at the ceiling. The tears never really stopped; they just took a break now and then. Eventually, fatigue triumphed, and he fell into the deepest, longest sleep he had had in ages. He woke up around 5:30 the next morning. The house was still. A low buzz emanated from each room as the women enjoyed their REM sleep. Solomon was starving. He shuffled downstairs to warm up his leftovers. It had been almost twenty-four hours since he ate anything—even longer since he had had a full meal—and his mental and emotional turbulence during that span had sapped just as much energy as if he had run five miles. . . uphill . . .

backwards.

On his way to the kitchen, he suddenly stopped. His stomach wanted to move forward, but his legs just didn't respond. Instead, Solomon turned slowly, as if someone were manually rotating his body. The Lord's Room stood before him, drawing him in. It was nearly a year since he had been in there, and now it was almost calling to him. Despite his hunger, Solomon stepped forward into his former fortress of solitude.

There was an eerie coolness to the room, cooler than the rest of the house. His suit of armor hung undisturbed under a plastic drycleaner's wrap, his clergy collar conspicuously absent. Grammy had the suit cleaned after that day in court, not realizing Solomon wouldn't be needing it any time soon, if ever. His Bible lay open on the desk. Solomon smiled as he pictured Simone sitting there reading the scriptures. The pillow he used to kneel on was laid neatly on the small sofa. *Her young knees could handle the floor better than mine*, he thought. He walked over to the Bible and thumbed through a few pages. The scriptures he had underlined in blue ink were now augmented by Simone's pink highlights. He stopped on a random page and read the scripture Simone had highlighted: "Man who is born of woman is of few days and full of trouble. He comes forth like a flower and fades away; he flees like a shadow and does not continue."

The apropos nature of the scripture did not escape Solomon, and he knew enough not to dismiss it as mere coincidence. At that moment, a hunger pang reminded him of his original mission. He closed the book and turned to leave The Lord's Room, still mulling over that verse that the Holy Spirit had led him to. As he put his hand on the door to close it behind him, his legs suddenly stopped again. There was a full-on tug of war, with his mind and stomach on one end, and his spirit on the other. And for the first time in forever, his spirit was winning. He couldn't leave, not yet. Solomon turned back and gently closed the door. He grabbed the pillow from the sofa and placed it on the floor. Slowly, he knelt down, closed his eyes and began to pray.

"Lord, I know You're there. I know You're always listening. I don't know how I've fallen so far. I don't know how to get back to where I'm supposed to be. It just feels like something in me shattered that day, and I don't know how to put it back together. I'm sorry, Lord. A man's days are 'full of trouble.' My days have been full of trouble. I need you. Please help me figure this out. I want to feel your presence like I used to. I want to be on fire like I used to be. Please help me get right again. In Jesus' name I pray, Amen."

Solomon didn't have any more words to say, but he couldn't get up. Not because of some miraculous thunderous voice telling him to be still or some mind-blowing revelation that God was downloading to him. No, Solomon couldn't get up because, for the first time in forever, he felt an overwhelming sense of peace envelop him. He felt the chill in the air disappear. The pain in his stomach withered away. The dull dehydration-induced headache subsided. And he could swear he felt the lightest touch on his shoulder. He dared not look for fear of losing the moment. It was the same feeling he felt as a boy after a tough loss, when his dad would put his hands on his shoulder and say, "It's gonna be alright son. We're not meant to win every fight. If we did, we'd never learn a thing." Solomon leaned his head slightly to the right, as if resting his head against the body of the unseen Comforter. No words necessary. Sometimes you just need a good hug from your Father.

A while later, Solomon emerged from The Lord's Room feeling lighter, not because of the total lack of food in his system, but because of the loving embrace he had just felt. Hope and peace had replaced his anger, confusion and despondency. He glided to the kitchen to finally deal with the hunger pains that had returned with a vengeance. The leftovers still smelled good enough to eat, and since it was the fastest way to get something hot and hearty down, he threw them in the microwave and downed a glass of water as he waited. Two days ago, he would have been impatiently barking at the microwave to hurry up. Now, after his meeting with God, he was totally at ease. Solomon whispered, "Thank you" as the ding of the microwave announced day-old breakfast was served.

As he sat down to eat, Solomon thought he heard a knock at the door. He ignored it because satisfying his hunger was far more important. Besides, nobody stops by at six in the morning. His first bite tasted like a Michelin-rated chef cooked it. *Best leftovers ever!* The culinary bliss was interrupted by another knock at the door. *Who in the world is at my door this early in the morning?* Solomon walked to the door, irritated that someone was interrupting his long-awaited meal.

"Who is it?" he called through the door.

"Good morning, Solomon. It's Gabby."

"Gabby?" Solomon opened the door. "What are you doing here? It's six in the morning."

"Hop in the car, and I'll tell you all about it," Gabby answered.

"You kiddin' me? I just sat down to eat for the first time in almost two days. And, by the way, it's six in the freakin' morning!"

Solomon's abrasive response surprised Gabby. She paused to collect herself and then continued. "I know and I apologize, Solomon. Are you eating the leftovers from yesterday?"

"Yes, I am." Solomon snapped back, then he finally remembered the spark he had rekindled just a few minutes earlier. "I'm sorry, Gabby. I'm a little cranky in the morning, and I'm downright mean when I'm hungry, so you definitely caught me at my worst. Please forgive my rudeness. I truly appreciate your concern, but I had a breakthrough this morning! For the first time in a long time, I felt peace. I felt connected to the Lord again. And it's because of you. Thank you so much. Would you like to come in?"

"I forgive you," Gabby replied, "and I understand. Not everyone is a morning person. That is wonderful! Praise God! You can tell me all about it on the way."

Solomon responded, "On the way? But I just sat down to eat."

"Well, we took your food to-go yesterday; you can eat it on-the-go today. I don't mind if you eat in the car. Will you come?" She turned around and walked back to her car. Solomon stood there stunned and, once again, felt compelled to accept her invitation. So, he closed the door, took another bite of his food and ran upstairs to throw on some clothes. Five minutes later, he walked out the front door holding the to-go plate and chewing another bite. Gabby was in her car idling in front of the gate, her head bowed low in prayer. Solomon quietly got in the car, but Gabby didn't budge. They sat for a minute or two, car idling, him eating and her praying, until she finally lifted her head, gave him a smile and headed down the road.

The sun had risen fully, with yellowish hues illuminating the path ahead. Solomon's meal was half devoured, even though he had taken only a few bites. It wasn't humanly possible to get it into his stomach fast enough, so each bite was a heaping mound of day-old delight. Solomon was too hungry to worry about impolitely talking with food in his mouth. At this point, he just didn't want to spit the food out bit by bit as he spoke. Besides, this was her idea in the first place. If she wanted polite Solomon, she should have waited until after breakfast.

"So, where are we going? And why are we going there so early?" Solomon asked, with a playful, curious tone.

"I'll answer the second question first. Every morning I wake up at 5:30 a.m. and spend an hour in God's presence. Some days I pray; some days I praise and worship; some days I just sit and listen. Today was a prayer day, and you were heavy on my spirit, so I started lifting you up, interceding for you. Then, I felt the Holy Spirit tell me to get up and go. I'm not one to come over to someone's house unannounced, especially a man, especially this early in the morning. But when the Lord tells you to go now, you don't barter for a more convenient time. You get up and go. So here I am."

"And the first question?"

"Your guess is as good as mine. The Lord told me to come get you; he hasn't told me the rest."

Solomon was astonished. It was rare to come across someone so totally devoted to God's will that they would drop everything and go, with only some sketchy details of His plan. And then it hit him. "Whoa. I think I know why He hasn't told you. This morning I spent some quality time with Him too. Not too much praying, mostly meditating and listening. At one point, a place popped into my head, and I felt this tug to go. I dismissed it at the time, thinking I had allowed my mind to wander off a bit. But, hearing you now, I know it was the Holy Spirit."

"So, where are we going?" Gabby asked.

"I need to introduce you to my wife, Gloria."

"Oh, you're married?"

"I was. She passed away a few years ago."

"Oh no. I am so sorry for your loss, Solomon. Point me in the right direction."

"She's buried at the cemetery about two miles past the church."

"Got it. We'll be there in a bit. In the meantime, tell me about what happened this morning."

"I woke up lighter this morning," Solomon began, his words slightly muffled by the pile of dough and syrup stuffed in each cheek. "I was all cried out, and fully awake, since I passed out early in the evening yesterday. When I came downstairs, I was pulled into my prayer room. I hadn't been in there for a long time. The Spirit wouldn't let me leave without praying, and for the first time in ages, I felt the presence of the Lord. I felt Him there, listening to me, even comforting me. There was an indescribable peace, a serenity that I didn't want to leave. And if it hadn't been for the hunger pains, I wouldn't have left."

Gabby smiled widely. "Create in me a clean heart, O God; and renew a right spirit within me.' Isn't God amazing? Such amazing love for us. We come to Him with a truly repentant heart, a heart that yearns for Him, and He'll be right there with arms wide open. I praise God for you, Solomon. I'm curious. Why do you think this morning was different from all the others over the last year?"

The question perplexed Solomon. Gabby had a knack for asking questions that required him to trek into a location he rarely traversed—his own heart. Solomon the clergyman was always focused on shepherding his little sheep; Solomon the family man needed to be the strong head his ladies could always look to for guidance, reassurance and security; Solomon the soldier couldn't waste time on introspection, with sergeants barking orders and bullets whizzing past. So rather than go to the rarely charted territory within, he dusted off his old liturgical doctrine and let Solomon the clergyman handle this one.

"Well, the Lord is 'longsuffering toward us, not willing that any should perish, but that all should come to repentance.' This morning He showed His love by forgiving me and embracing me again, but He also showed His omnipotence by drawing me in and onto my knees. He basically said, 'That's enough wallowing in the mud, Solly. Time to get up and come home.' "

Gabby's normally pleasant countenance faded into a stern intensity that Solomon had not seen in her before. She pulled over to the side of the road, put the car in park, and turned in her seat so she could face him.

"Solomon, the Lord has never stopped embracing you. He's not sitting up there in heaven with a stopwatch saying, 'OK, it's about time for me to make Solomon come back home.' That is not the God we serve. He is not the author of confusion. The enemy and his servants are. We are. A man of the cloth doesn't lay down his cross unless there is some chaos going on in the one place you seem unwilling to look." Gabby lifted her hand purposefully, with her finger pointing to Solomon's chest.

"Yesterday," Gabby continued, "you were full of tears, full of pain, full of anger. Do you really think a day of crying and some good sleep made all that evaporate overnight? Letting the faucet run all day emptied just enough pain from your secret place for your spirit to finally see the light of day. The Holy Spirit didn't suddenly reappear to draw you into your prayer room this morning. He never stopped calling you, Solomon. You just stopped listening, because your flesh had taken over. It was your spirit that could finally grab hold of Him again. It was your spirit that refused to spend another day disconnected from Him. God was lovingly patient enough for you to exit the pigpen and start the journey home. Just like the prodigal son, He saw you a long way off and came to meet you, but you are not home yet. You gotta keep digging, Solomon. You cried a river yesterday, but there's a sea of tears buried in you that will surface again. Hear me now, my friend: you will be tried again, and if you do not deal with the roots of your pain now, you will find yourself back in that pigpen, and you will not find your way home."

The words chilled Solomon to his very core. He couldn't speak; his tongue felt glued to the roof of his mouth. It was not often that someone received a prophetic word. It was one thing to read about such divine occurrences and believe they could happen, but it was an otherworldly, mind-boggling experience when you become the target of the prophetic utterance. For Solomon, it was the first time God hand-delivered His word to him. And for that word to be so direct, so unequivocal and so ominous, it made Solomon awash in the fear of the Lord. Once again, he lost his appetite. Thankfully, he had only a couple of bites left. As Solomon closed his takeout plate, Gabby turned, shifted to drive and continued down the road.

12

"O My Father, if it is possible, let this cup pass from Me; nevertheless, not as I will, but as You will."

Matthew 26:39

God's word hovered in the car like a fog. Solomon and Gabby sat silently for a while, as she continued toward Gloria's resting place. This wasn't uncomfortable silence; it was an unspoken agreement to let God's prophetic word exist, without competition or clutter. All of sudden, another one of his dad's proverbs came to mind: "If you fail a test, you don't get a beer and a pat on the back; you get to take the class over again." Solomon's mind raced through a labyrinth of thoughts. *Why would God test me by allowing something so terrible to happen to someone so innocent? What's coming next? Is my other daughter in the cross hairs? I can't fail again. If I don't make it back home next time, where will I end up? What does He mean by "keep digging"?*

As if on spiritual cue, Gabby broke the silence and said, "So, tell me about your wife."

The question immediately yanked his thoughts from the maze. Solomon didn't talk about Gloria with anyone outside the family.

Every year on her birthday, he and the girls baked a cake and drove to her grave to celebrate, but instead of counting the years since her birth, the cake read "Welcome Home" and displayed the years since the day she went home to glory. In a few months, it would be home-going celebration number 9.

"She was the love of my life," Solomon began. "We met in the seventh grade. She was good at everything! We got married pretty soon after we graduated from college. They say marriage isn't easy, and they're right. But in our case, my wife didn't make it tough; life took care of that. Gloria turned the lemons life threw at us into lemonade."

"I've never been married," Gabby responded. "She sounds like the kind of wife I would strive to be. Did she and your mother get along?"

Solomon laughed at the question. "Did they? For a while, they got along better than my mother and I did." They both laughed. The levity was a welcome break from the weight of the moment.

"What is your favorite memory of her?"

"Wow. Just one?" Solomon started to ponder the seemingly herculean task of finding the single, best needle in a stack of needles, then quickly realized there was only one real choice. "Hmm, there are so many awesome times we had, but I gotta say it was a family day in 2005. The girls were so young. Bethany wasn't even six years old. The two of us got up very early on a Saturday morning. We loaded the girls into the car and drove to the lookout on Mount Quigley to watch the sun rise. There is this big flat rock up there. We laid our blanket out on it and had a sunrise breakfast picnic. We told stories and laughed a lot. I loved her laugh. Then we drove down to the valley, pulled out some makeshift cardboard sleds I put together and raced down the big grassy hill. We rolled around a bunch; I tossed the girls all around.

"It was two days before I deployed for Iraq. To this day, they still call it the best day ever. And they're right! Gloria was never more perfect than on that day. I enjoyed every second. I studied every line that formed on the edges of her smile. I counted every eyelash. I memorized the way her ears peeked out from under her pretty hair. It was our best day."

"Oh my. I can just picture it!" Gabby responded. "It's amazing how the uncertainty of life can make us so in tune and appreciative of the special moments. Remember that big storm last fall?"

"Of course," Solomon replied.

"Storms like that scare me, but they also make me aware of just how little I am in the grand scheme of things. That wind was so strong, it knocked down trees, flipped semis on the highway. It could have been the tree outside my home or the truck I sped past to get home. I remember everything about that day. I saw fifteen lightning flashes; the strongest gust was sixty-two miles per hour; seven inches of rain fell that day. And Houston beat Cleveland 31-17."

"Ouch! And I thought we were friends!" Solomon and Gabby both laughed again.

"Friends can tell each other the truth. And the truth is, Solomon, the Browns were terrible last year. It definitely sounds like you found the rib that God prepared for you. What is the worst memory of your time with Gloria?"

Immediately, the wind was sucked out of Solomon's sails. Levity devolved into agitation. Solomon rarely ventured into this dismal part of his past. There were so many wonderful moments in his years with Gloria, why spoil the joy of those years by spending even a millisecond thinking about the last eighteen months of their life together?

"Gabby," Solomon said with a calm, arctic coldness. "That's a button you shouldn't push. Some closets you don't open. You're knocking on the door to one of them."

For the first time, Gabby didn't push further. She knew the question she asked would cross a threshold for Solomon, but she also knew that the Holy Spirit was in charge, and if He put that question on her heart, then it must be asked. And now, He was leading her to be silent. Whatever happened next was between Him and Solomon. Gabby and Solomon sat quietly the rest of the way to the graveyard.

When they arrived at the main entrance, Gabby asked, "Should I turn here?"

"Keep straight," Solomon responded, his voice an unsettling blend of apprehension, anger and sorrow. "The road will wind left. I'll let you know when to park." After a few more seconds of silence, Solomon directed her over to a curbside parking spot.

Gabby turned off the engine then reached over and gently held Solomon's hand. She said, "Solomon, I am truly honored to meet your Gloria." Solomon said nothing. Rather than look her way, he gave a gentle, reassuring squeeze, then lowered his head. The weight of the moment forced Solomon to gird up his loins for what was to come. Decades earlier, before a big game, Solomon would disappear into a lonely corner of the room to focus all his energy on the enormity of the challenge that lay ahead. This was such a moment, and his passenger seat would have to do.

As Gabby exited the car, Solomon stayed still, his head down and eyes closed. He wasn't praying; he wasn't resting. He was preparing his mind, heart and soul for the challenge that was sure to confront him. A day earlier, he was blindsided by the rogue wave of emotions that overcame him. So, it was now time to get mentally and emotionally ready so that he wouldn't devolve into a blubbering mess again.

Gabby patiently waited outside the car, trusting that Solomon would emerge, without prompting, when he was good and ready. Eventually, he lifted his head, opened the door and stepped out. "This way."

"You loved your wife very much, Solomon. For her to have gone home so many years ago, yet the loss is still so raw for you today. That love is so precious, so priceless."

Solomon didn't respond. It was clear Gabby thought Solomon's somber mood was caused by his impending arrival at Gloria's grave. But there was something else going on within him. During the long period of silence after Gabby asked about his worst memory of Gloria, the words "keep digging" kept pulsing in his head. And, this time, he knew exactly what it meant. The Holy Spirit was telling him to open that painful closet, to break the seal on the last eighteen months of Gloria's life. As angry as it made him to be forced to dredge up those memories, he couldn't back down now. *You're not home yet, Solly. Keep digging.*

About thirty yards down a winding path stood a beautiful onyx headstone with the name "Gloria Cooper Trudeau" engraved above a silver cross. Solomon walked up to the gravestone; Gabby stopped a few feet farther back. Solomon knelt down, kissed his fingers and gently placed them on the face of the headstone. He spoke softly to the tombstone: "Hey, honey, I love you and I miss you. I'm sorry I haven't come to see you in so long. I've been in a fog for a little while now. That thing with Simone really knocked me for a loop. I know I should have been thankful that she fought him off before he could get what he wanted, but I couldn't see past my anger. I'm ashamed to tell you this, but I beat up a kid the other day, just because he was tryin' to talk to Bethany. It's been a really dark year on this side. But I'm startin' to see the Light again.

"I brought a friend of mine. Well, she brought me. We're not dating or anything, but I did lean in that direction when I first saw her. I'm pretty sure God sent her to help me get right again. So, I'm gonna tell her about us and about—" Solomon paused and dropped his head low for a few moments. Then he felt a gentle comforting hand on his shoulder, a reassuring squeeze from which he drew strength to continue. "Lord's telling me to dig up the pain I've buried all these years. So, I'm gonna tell her about us now."

"Gabby," Solomon said quietly, still kneeling before the headstone. Silence. Solomon still felt her hand on his shoulder, so he said her name again softly, "Gabby." Silence. He lifted his head and looked over his shoulder and was shocked to see Gabby still standing at least eight feet back, her head down and eyes closed in prayer. As he realized whose gentle, comforting hand he had felt on his shoulder, tears began to pool in his eyes.

When Gabby lifted her head and opened her eyes, Solomon motioned for her to come closer. "Please, I'd like to introduce you to my wife." Gabby walked forward and stood next to him. "I met my wife, Gloria, in middle school. I knew she was special the minute I saw her. There was something amazing about the way she made me feel. It wasn't some love-sick puppy feeling, even though I definitely was that. It's kinda hard to describe.

"I used to mow lawns on weekends for money when I was a kid. I'd mow as fast as I could to get as many lawns done as possible before noon. Some days, I'd do as many as ten lawns in a morning. I wasn't too particular, and, honestly, I wasn't very conscientious. I worked hard, but I was more concerned with quantity than quality, you know what I mean? Well, there was this one house about three blocks down that never let me do their lawn. It was the biggest, nicest house around. The yard was beautiful; the porch was always clean; hedges always neatly manicured. Of all the houses I did, that was the one house I always wanted. One day, the owner hired me—I think his landscaper was out of town that week. I spent twice as long mowing that lawn as I usually did. The owner paid me more than the others only because of the size of the lawn, but that wasn't my motivation, surprisingly enough. I just felt like this yard was so special, I couldn't be the one that diminished it. I felt like I couldn't let the owner down because he had entrusted his beautiful yard to me. I'm not comparing Gloria to yard work, but it's the best way I can describe the feeling I had every minute I was with her. Something in me treasured her so much that I wanted to be *more* in every way—more loving, more trustworthy, more hardworking, more faithful, more saved. I wanted to be her Superman, her knight in shining armor. Being with my wife inspired me to be the best man I could be, and that made me love her even more. She was hot, too, so that didn't hurt."

"Sounds like you found your rib," Gabby said.

"I found my rib, my heart and my backbone. I feel her even as I'm talking to you. She was always right there when I needed her the most—always right there." Solomon paused and grinned. "Gloria died nine years ago from breast cancer. You asked what was the worst memory. It wasn't the day she died. We all could see her decline. It was long and painful. Near the end, we all knew it was time.

"One of my favorite sportscasters was Stuart Scott; he died from cancer too. He said, 'When you die, it does not mean that you lose to cancer. You beat cancer by how you live, why you live and in the manner in which you live.' By that definition, she kicked cancer's butt, by the way she fought, the way she lived her life and the way she loved others. It was just her time. Seeing her lying peacefully—no more pain, no more fighting—I knew she was a million times better off. I was sad, of course. I'm still sad to this day, but I wasn't selfish enough to want her to stay and keep suffering.

"No. The worst memory I have of my years with Gloria was the moment I discovered that lump in her breast. She fought for a year and half after that day. I held her every day as her body ached. I sat next to her on the bathroom floor as her stomach refused to keep anything in. I took her shopping for head wraps to cover the patches, then shaved it all when she had had enough of the patchwork. I held my girls and explained to them that their mother wasn't going to be with us much longer. I kissed her goodbye as she closed her eyes for the last time. Still, the worst day of my life was when I found that lump. I tried to be strong for her—show no fear, show unshakable faith. But the second I found that lump, I just knew this road wasn't gonna end at happily ever after—not anymore. I knew my wife would be gone sooner than I ever imagined. Despite all the praying, I knew my wife was gonna die the day I found that lump."

Solomon crumbled to the ground, sobbing. Gabby followed him down and put her arm around him. She, too, had to wipe her own tears away.

"It's killing me! It's been killing me since the day she died. I mean, how could I have let her down like that! I was a frickin' pastor! Hezekiah prayed, and the Lord gave him fifteen more years! Every single one of our prayers had my unbelief weighing it down. Every time I said 'We're gonna beat this', I felt in my heart I was lying to her face, to my kids' faces. The church held a special corporate prayer just for her. I stood there all pious-looking, but I didn't think it would work, not one bit. What kind of husband, what kind of father, what kind of minister gives his wife up for dead—" The boulder in his throat interrupted the thought. "What kind of minister gives his wife up for dead before she's even diagnosed?"

Gabby held Solomon as he wept. It wasn't time to talk. Solomon had so many tears in him, and she just needed to be there with him and help him cry.

Morning was full-grown now. The low buzz of a slow-moving car occasionally broke the silence, those inside melting with compassion for the grief-stricken pair, whom they assumed must have just lost a loved one. The third car to pass by nudged Solomon from his tears after nearly ten minutes of lamentation. He lifted his head and sat down on the grass in front of Gloria's headstone. Gabby followed suit.

Solomon swallowed hard, and kept digging. "Truth be told, every day of those eighteen months loosened the clergy collar around my neck. Not because of what my wife suffered, but because of hypocrisy. Teaching Sunday school, preaching sermons and leading prayer meetings, knowing I don't have enough faith in the very Word I'm proclaiming to apply it to the love of my life! When she finally went home, I had a hard time believing. Not in God, but in myself as a man of God.

"Losing my collar that day in the courtroom was the culmination of what I had been feeling for some time already. I started the walk away from the pulpit years earlier, so when my collar fell, I didn't have anything left to pick it up."

"And you've been in this fog ever since," Gabby interjected. "The time you spent with God this morning was the first good meal you've had in a year, Solomon."

She now sat straight up, eyes fixed on his. Her empathetic, comforting presence evaporated into a steely-eyed glare and intense aura. "You know what the word says. God's gifts and calling are without repentance. You can set fire to your black suit and bury that collar, but it won't change who the Lord called you to be, and it won't nullify the marrow-deep desire within you to be connected to Him. It's like fire shut up in your bones, but instead of letting it pull you towards Him, you doused His fire in a river of grief, doubt and pain."

"Yeah," Solomon sighed. "I know. I guess you're done with the weeping willow over here. Me too."

"Iron sharpens iron, Solomon," Gabby continued. "I'm not a man, but I'm not a marshmallow either. Don't get me wrong. I'm sure you have a few more rivers to cry before you're done, but now isn't the time for that. We gotta figure out some things here so those rivers lead to some healing. Did you talk to anyone? Your pastor? Your mother? Anyone?"

"No," Solomon answered. "I took it to God in prayer. Pastor Jefferson was always available. He called me into his office a couple of times to just talk, but I never let him know what was really going on in this head of mine."

"Why not?" Gabby asked. "If anyone could help you deal with the confusion and pain you were going through, I would think your pastor would be at the top of the list."

Solomon paused. She was right. Why didn't he confide in Pastor Jefferson, supposedly his friend? It had been so long that he needed to think, meditate even, on the answer. *Keep digging, Solly.* "Well, I've never been one to ask for help. And I didn't know how to tell my pastor that his youth pastor didn't think any of the prayers he was praying for his wife to recover would work. You are the only person I have ever told."

"Solomon, God did add more years to Hezekiah's life, but that's not always the case. Sometimes, His answer is 'No.' I won't tell you I know for sure that Gloria's time had come, or that God would've healed her if unbelief hadn't, as you describe it, weighed down your prayers. I do know that God allows things to happen in our lives for reasons we may never know. And sometimes He allows us to see the end at the very beginning. Did you ask Him, 'Is this illness unto death?' "

"No," Solomon replied. "I couldn't bring myself to ask that. I guess I didn't want Him to confirm the worst. I just wanted to keep fighting for my wife and hope someone's prayers were getting through."

Gabby said, "Only God knows if Gloria's end could have been postponed. That being said, either you stand on His word, or you don't. And it's when the really tough times hit that we find out what we truly stand on." Gabby stopped at that moment to measure her words. "You said you wanted to be her Superman. What did you mean?"

Solomon smiled at the question. He remembered how it felt when he rose to whatever occasion his wife needed him to; how she hugged him tight when he changed her spark plugs; how she beamed from ear to ear when he worked with Brittany all week to do her presentation at the school-wide assembly; how she held his arm tight when they walked past those punks loitering outside the ice cream parlor. "Whatever she needed me to be, I wanted to be that and then some. That's what I meant."

"I think every good husband wants to be a hero in his wife's eyes," Gabby said, as they lightened the atmosphere with a little laugh. "Speaking as a woman, though, we want a good man, not Superman. We want a faithful, loving husband, not Superman. We want a dedicated father to our kids, not Superman. Solomon, you were never meant to be her Superman, because she already had the Son of Man. You can never be all that He is, yet it sounds like you put that totally unrealistic pressure on yourself. I guess it worked out most of the time, but when the big test hit, it sent you reeling. No man can be all things to someone, except the Son of Man. Solomon, when it came time for you to stand on His word and your faith, you fell short. And it's not because you didn't believe. You spent so much time unwittingly trying to be who He is to her that you forgot how to be who she needed you to be: her covering. You built a beautiful house on sand, and when the earth shook, your house cracked. And when it shook again, your house crumbled."

Solomon bristled at her words. "Hold on, Gabby. Every man

worth his salt wants to be his family's knight in shining armor. That's just how we're made. Me wanting to be the best husband and dad ever motivated me to be a better man and keep growing. I don't see how that's a bad thing and definitely don't see how that could lead to a crisis of faith."

"You're right. Any woman with some sense would fall on her knees and thank God daily for a husband who loved her the way you loved Gloria. And you wanting to be the best husband ever is not a bad thing at all! Let me ask you something, though. When your girls came to you crying with a broken toy in their hands, what did you do?"

"I fixed it," Solomon answered, puzzled by the ridiculously obvious question.

"When your mother got less and less able to care for herself, was it hard for you to ask her to move in?"

Solomon's chest expanded as if pride were being pumped into his lungs by a blower. "Not in the least!"

"And when Gloria asked you to put some new doodad together, I bet you handled it, no problem."

"Yeah, there was always something to fix or put together on the 'honey-do' list. I remember Gloria bought this futon online. She didn't realize you had to assemble it yourself—I should say myself! That thing was a pain in the butt! It was made from solid wood and had a thousand different screws, washers and nuts. It took me three hours, with her standing over my shoulder to make sure I didn't scratch it."

"That's what I'm talking about!" Gabby said, with a nice laugh. "You are a really good father, a really good son and the kind of husband women pray for."

With that Gabby paused and looked deeply into Solomon's eyes. They both were silent, and Solomon's mind started to imagine something he hadn't pondered with any depth before—loving another woman. In a few days, the woman before him had meant more to him than any woman since Gloria's passing. *Maybe she is the angel God sent to fill the void Gloria left in my life. But who wants to be with a broken-down, fallen preacher? Maybe that's why she's working so hard to fix me up.* As Solomon started to lean forward ever so slightly, Gabby brought his fairytale postulation to an abrupt end.

"And when she fell ill, how did it feel when you couldn't fix it?" Gabby let the question hang in the air like the smell of burnt toast —acrid, jarring, disappointing. "Some things can't be fixed by you, aren't even meant to be fixed by you. What glory is left for God if you could fix everything? But the One who could fix it, you weren't able to truly call on. You spent so much time and energy being your family's 'Superman,' you failed to truly root your faith in the one, true super Man. So, when He sent the mother of all tests, your faith fell short. It's possible to be everything your family *wants* you to be and miss the most important thing they *need* you to be—the priest of the home. And, sometimes, preachers spend so much time preaching to others, they forget they're also preaching to themselves. I think you can drink from both of those cups, Solomon."

Come on! Can't a guy feel good for thirty seconds? Solomon sat there stone-faced. His pride wouldn't let him acknowledge openly what he knew in his heart—Gabby was right. He knew he fell short spiritually in that tragic season, but he never understood, or even asked, why he fell short. Now he started to realize the fall wasn't just in the moment; it had been slowly building up momentum like a runaway train without a conductor.

After what seemed like an eternity, Solomon muttered, "Keep digging, keep digging."

"What?" Gabby asked.

"Nothing. Gabby, I will never apologize for trying to be the best husband and dad I could be. Never. But I can't argue with what you said. I know we should trust in the Lord with all our hearts and lean not on our own understanding. I know we're supposed to cast all of our cares upon Him. And I know that, for some reason, I didn't. For some reason, I couldn't. I just don't know the reason. Don't get me wrong, I never lost my faith in Jesus. But I never put all of my trust in Him. So, what keeps ringing in my head is 'keep digging.' But can we put the shovels down for now? We are in a graveyard, you know."

Gabby laughed lightly, recognizing what Solomon meant—it was time to go.

For the entire ride home, Solomon and Gabby had the most pleasant, non-emotional, non-gut-wrenching conversation they had had since the day they met on the side of the road. They laughed about the crazy things kids do and debated the state of the union. They even argued over who was the best quarterback of all time (Solomon was stuck on Otto Graham, while Gabby insisted it was Joe Montana). Neither of them brought up the more pressing matters, which allowed Solomon to just feel—good.

13

"For thus says the One who is high and lifted up, who inhabits eternity, whose name is Holy: 'I dwell in the high and holy place, and also with him who is of a contrite and lowly spirit, to revive the spirit of the lowly, and to revive the heart of the contrite.' "

Isaiah 57:15

The house smelled like a man's morning paradise: The top note was a teaser of fresh biscuits. There was a hint of marmalade that brought sweet freshness to the mix. But the pièce de résistance was the invigorating, almost primal smell of perfectly cooked bacon! As Solomon's dad used to say, "The only good thing about Noah's flood—besides the eight that made it—was God let us have bacon after that!" Grammy hadn't disturbed Solomon after he closed the door to his room yesterday, so her motherly instincts to take care of her "baby" boy had not assuaged. She had gotten up no more than fifteen minutes after Solomon had left and assumed he had gone on an early-morning walk. So she set about making a nice, hearty breakfast to greet him when he returned. She made his plate and covered it up and waited anxiously for his return.

Simone woke up to the sound (and intoxicating smell) of sizzling bacon. "Where's Daddy?" she asked Grammy when she entered the kitchen.

"Probably went for a walk. Are you hungry?"

"Oh, yes, I am!"

The two made their plates and sat together. Bethany walked in just as they sat down. "Good morning, family. Grammy, thank you soooo much for cooking breakfast. I'm starving!"

"Grab a plate then, honey. Your father should be back any minute now," Grammy replied.

"Perfect, 'cause I need to talk about Friday night," Bethany continued. "That was not cool! I mean, I didn't like the guy, but Daddy didn't need to go all fight club on him! I'm in college. I'm allowed to talk to guys, and they can talk to me. I can handle myself!"

Grammy looked up at her perturbed, legally grown but mentally immature granddaughter with love and the sage understanding that comes with seeing the world as a septuagenarian. "Baby, you are nineteen years old. That means you are old enough to be on your own. But you are *not* grown. There is so much you don't know. If we weren't looking after you and praying over you, God only knows what this nasty world would do to you. Let me show you something." Grammy didn't have anything material to show them, but Bethany and Simone knew that some story was soon to follow. "If you stand on the porch, what is the farthest you can see in any direction, Simone?"

Simone thought about it and said, "I got good eyes, probably to the top of the hill on Madison Street."

"That's pretty far," Grammy replied. "Bethany, if you were on top of the hill on Madison street, how far do you think you could see?"

"Really, Grammy? I mean, we've got serious stuff to deal with and you want me to take an imaginary vision test?"

Grammy didn't say a word. She just maintained her loving, expectant gaze.

"Probably five miles," Bethany answered as she punished a biscuit with a vicious chomp.

"When we go up into the mountains, we can see the whole city, right?"

"Yes, Grammy," both ladies replied.

"When you flew home, Bethany, did the pilot announce any sights to see out the window?"

Bethany shrugged, not willing to put any energy into trying to remember an announcement on a flight she slept through days ago.

"Well, once I flew from Chicago to L.A. About an hour in, the pilot said we could see Denver if we looked out the right side, and Colorado Springs if we looked out the left. Do you see what I'm getting at?" Grammy asked.

"I think so, Grammy," Simone replied. Bethany was starting to get the picture, but her pride and desire to remain pissed off wouldn't let her acknowledge it.

"The higher you go, the more you see. Life is the same. The older you get, the more you see. Child, you are old enough to start learning *how* to see, but you got a lot more years before you *do* see. Let us do our job to protect and guide you until you start seeing the forest AND the trees." Grammy's loving, gentle countenance morphed into an intense, ominous glare. "Now, your father protected you Friday night. No, he shouldn't have hit the boy, but don't you ever get mad at a man protecting his daughter! There's a battle going on inside your daddy. It's spiritual; it's emotional. God is not through with him yet. He needs us to love him, not judge him, not condemn him. And I'm the only one allowed to scold him. We will talk about what happened Friday night, and you will not dishonor your daddy. Do you understand?" She seemed to grow, in that moment, into a frighteningly powerful old woman, whom one should not cross.

"Yes, Grammy," both ladies replied in unison.

"Good. Let's enjoy breakfast. Your father should be here soon."

But when breakfast was over, Solomon still hadn't arrived. The girls did the dishes, while Grammy sat at the table, sipping her tea. After everything was cleaned up, Grammy went upstairs to shower the morning residue away. She always felt the greasy stench of bacon lingered long after its tantalizing aroma had passed. When she came downstairs, forty-five minutes later, her "baby boy' " was still not there.

"Did either of you talk to your daddy yesterday?" Grammy asked.

"No, Grammy, not a word," Bethany answered. Simone shook her head.

"Well, did he say anything to you?"

"No, Grammy," they both replied.

"Did you type him?"

Simone couldn't help but giggle at the oh-so-behind-the-times question as Bethany answered, "Yes, Grammy, I texted him and called twice while you were upstairs, but they went straight to voicemail."

"He's not gonna go for a two-hour walk this early in the morning. He definitely wasn't himself yesterday. I don't want him walking on the side of the road in that state. Honey, would you mind driving me to go look for him?"

"I'm going too!" Simone demanded.

"Oh no you're not. You will stay right here, just in case he returns while we're out. Call your sister if he does."

As they grabbed their coats, they heard Solomon's heavy steps coming up the front stairs. Grammy skipped to the door, her relief and joy evident in how quickly she covered the distance. She opened the door as Solomon was getting the keys out of his pocket—a process he was intentionally elongating. Solomon knew disapproving looks, tough questions and a sharp rebuke awaited on the other side of that door, and he wasn't in a hurry to confront it.

"Hey, Mama." He hugged her tight, subconsciously recalling how therapeutic a good, long hug from Mama could be.

"Hi, baby. Did you have a nice walk?"

"I did a lot of thinking while I was out, a lot of praying. I wouldn't call it 'nice,' but it was necessary. Still got a lot of thoughts and feelings whizzing around up here," Solomon replied, as he tapped the side of his head.

Simone got up from the sofa and reached Solomon before Bethany, who was glad her dad was safe, but in no mood to be lovey-dovey.

"Hey, Daddy." Simone came close to give her hero a big hug.

"Hey, Dad." Bethany never called him "Daddy" when she was mad at him; it just seemed way too endearing. She leaned in to hug, knowing it was expected. Solomon was fully aware of the cold front emanating from his oldest daughter.

"Ladies, let's sit down for a bit."

Bethany immediately walked to a chair, ensuring nobody could sit next to her and interrupt her God-given right to be pissed off. There was so much she wanted to say, but one look from Grammy reminded her to hold her tongue.

"I am so sorry for the way I acted Friday night. I am so ashamed. There is no excuse for what I did. That boy I attacked deserved to be straightened out, but he didn't deserve to be assaulted. You didn't deserve to have me ruin our Family Movie Night. You didn't deserve to be humiliated by my terrible lapse in self-control. And, Bethany, you didn't deserve to have me treat you like a little girl and then run through you while trying to get to him! You will always be my little girl, but you are not a little girl. I should have trusted you to handle the situation, because I raised you to handle those situations. I'm just so, so sorry."

Solomon's eyes began to water. At that moment, Bethany couldn't even remember what she was mad about. Solomon's heartfelt apology was moving, but her daddy's tears took a blowtorch to that wall of ice she had erected. She ran toward Solomon and hugged him so tight, they both began to cry. The two embraced for a long time. Grammy held Simone's hand to keep her from interrupting the cathartic moment. This was more than forgiveness. This was a father reconnecting with his daughter. And that's something you do not rush.

As the two released one another, Grammy touched Solomon's shoulder gently and asked, "What did that poor boy do to set you off like that?" She already knew the boy's conduct wasn't the issue; she didn't know if Solomon understood that. She was surveying the course to see how deep in the rough her son was. If he started explaining how the boy did this and how the boy did that, then she would know that her son was still somewhere out of bounds, and she would have to roll up her maternal sleeves and get to work.

"Grammy, it's not what he did. To be honest, what twenty-year-old boy with 20/20 vision wouldn't put in overtime to be a part of this beautiful young lady's world?" No one could give a compliment like Solomon, and Bethany lapped it up like a dry sponge dropped in water. "No, it was me. There're some things I've been stewing on for a long, long time. It had nothing to do with him; it was me. That boy triggered some things in me that shouldn't be there. Wrath. Unforgiveness. Vengeance."

Grammy began to tear up now, not in sadness, but in gratitude. She knew her baby was finally starting to see the light. She knew her baby was finally getting up out of the pigpen and starting the journey back home. She knew her prayers were being answered. She closed her eyes, and her heart cried out, "Thank you, Jesus!"

"I didn't hit just that boy; I hit rock bottom. I sat in that cell all night just stewing over what I had done. How can I have so much rage in me that I don't even see my little girl, who I supposedly was running to rescue? How can I be so thirsty to hurt someone that I don't even care who I'm hurting? I can't stay in that place. I won't. I thank God He won't let me stay there. He sent someone, a friend. I've only known her for a few weeks, but she's helping me climb out of this hole I've been in."

"Honey," Grammy said with all the love a mother can muster, "your yesterday ain't nothing compared to your tomorrow. You're on a journey, son, and only God knows where it ends, but I am so proud of you for getting up and trusting Him again. Now, I did hear you say 'she,' right?"

"That's exactly what you heard," Simone answered with a nosy, playful grin. "How about you, B?"

"Yup. No doubt about it. Mystery friend is a mystery   l-a-d-y."

"Well," Grammy continued, "you're gonna have to invite this 'friend' over for dinner."

Solomon was immediately reminded of just how outnumbered he was. "Slow down, ladies. She's not *that* kind of friend; at least, I don't think she is. To be honest, for the first time in who knows how long—"

"I do!" Simone interrupted. "Too long!"

Solomon could only smile. The hot seat he had expected morphed into an entirely different type of awkwardness, but he felt much better equipped to handle this three-pronged heat wave. Solomon regained command of the discussion with a playful yet purposeful tone.

"To be honest, I wouldn't mind if she became *that* kind of friend, but we'll see what the Lord has planned. Either way, I think it's waaaaay too soon to be planning a family dinner with her. I'm starting to sweat, so I can only imagine what y'all would do to Gabby."

"Ah, so the mystery friend from God has a name," Grammy chimed in, playing along. "Well, you know what they say, if you can't stand the heat—"

"Get off the sofa!" Solomon finished. "Which is what I'm gonna do. Matter of fact, we all need to get up and start getting ready. Don't want to be late for service." It had always been part of the plan to go to church as a family on Sunday, but after the debacle at the movies, and with Solomon's recently tepid enthusiasm towards all things holy, they all assumed that today would be a nice quiet day at the house. The girls exchanged curiously excited looks as Solomon stood up.

"Will 'our' new friend be there?" Bethany yelled as Solomon disappeared up the stairs.

"Maybe."

14

"Behold, I stand at the door and knock. If anyone hears My voice and opens the door, I will come in to him and dine with him, and he with Me."

Revelation 3:20

It had been a while since the whole family went to Sunday service together. Simone and Grammy were there every Sunday, a few rows from the front. Solomon made it two or three times per month, but he usually drove separately and preferred his seat in the back row. Today, Solomon walked in the center of his family, Grammy holding his arm, Bethany holding his hand. For the first time in what seemed like forever, they looked like a family on one holy accord. Solomon walked his family to the steps with a sense of peace and pride. Even after the spectacle he made of himself Friday night, he no longer felt the weight of shame as he walked to the front doors.

He also was curious to see if Gabby was present; he didn't see her car as he parked. Despite the hot seat he had left this morning, he still secretly hoped she would be there. He wanted to introduce his family to the woman who had had such a profound impact on him in such a short time. But he didn't want to *look* like he was looking for her, so Solomon slyly kissed Grammy's forehead, using the opportunity to scan the right side of the parking lot. *Nope.* He turned and kissed Bethany as well, looking over her head to the left side of the lot. *Negatory.* He winked at Simone, using the opportunity to glance behind just to see if he missed her car. *Strike three.*

"Good morning. Don't y'all look absolutely priceless today!" Sister Strickland's familiar and pleasant voice greeted the Trudeaus at the steps. Some people are assigned and others are called; Sister Strickland was definitely called. She was the most hospitable, genuinely warm person in the congregation. Even when she was having a bad day, she still found a way to be authentically happy and pleasant with everyone. It's no wonder she was the primary greeter on Sundays. No one could make a better impression for the church than she.

"Look who's back! It's so good to see you, Bethany."

Bethany broke ranks and hugged her tightly. "It's good to see you again, Sister Strickland. You been keepin' an eye on these knuckleheads for me?"

"Oh, that's for sure!"

"Hello, my sister," Solomon said as he bent low to hug the amiable greeter.

"How you doin', Pastor Solomon? It always lifts my spirit to see you."

"Ditto." Solomon smiled broadly.

More warm smiles and polite hellos greeted the family as they entered the sanctuary, but the reality of the past two days fell upon Solomon like a flood. All of a sudden, the shame he didn't feel twenty-five feet ago now began to overtake him. He felt every kind greeting was followed by a whisper.

"Did you hear what happened on Friday?" "I thought he was in jail." "Can you believe he used to be a pastor?"

Oh, how Solomon wanted to plant himself in his usual spot right there in the back row. A few more smiling faces made him want to U-turn back to the car and call it a day. But he knew he couldn't. His family needed to be together today, to allow their unified worship to help knit them closer together after such a tumultuous weekend. So, despite the darts he imagined cloaked behind every glance, the Trudeaus proceeded to Simone and Grammy's regular spot—at the front of the church.

Pastor Jefferson was a bit more enthusiastic than normal this morning. After the choir finished, he broke out in song himself, leading the church in some extended praise. (When the pastor led worship songs, the whole church participated. It could be that the church followed his anointed leadership, or everyone was just as enthusiastic about how awesome God is, or that only Jesus would want to hear the pastor sing solo.) He normally preferred to speak from behind the pulpit, but today he chose to speak to the congregation from the floor.

"Bless the Lord, oh my soul and all that is within me. Bless His holy name. Amen?" the pastor began.

"Amen."

"Please join me in reading our scripture this morning, Hebrews Chapter 12, Verses 1 and 2.

'Therefore we also, since we are surrounded by so great a cloud of witnesses, let us lay aside every weight, and the sin which so easily ensnares us, and let us run with endurance the race that is set before us, looking unto Jesus, the author and finisher of our faith, who for the joy that was set before Him endured the cross, despising the shame, and has sat down at the right hand of the throne of God.'

"Please, be seated. Let me tell you a story about a young man in Chicago. This young man was prodigiously talented on a basketball court. He was also driven to maximize his God-given ability. He would stay in the park for hours on end, by himself, dribbling, doing lay-ups, practicing jump shots—preparing for a career in the game he was obsessed with, a career he just knew would happen. This young man was certainly ambitious. He was a five-foot-nine-inch eighth-grader with toothpicks for legs who would even practice slam dunks.

"He stood at midcourt, measuring the approach. Then he started running and dribbling, accelerating quickly, eyes focused on his prize, ten feet up. He started his ascent a foot in front of the free throw line, ball cupped in his relatively large hand. He rose, and rose, then swung his arm forward. WHACK! He slammed the ball on the front of the rim and landed on his backside. Some bystanders burst into laughter, telling the boy he should stick to jump shots. Sore, embarrassed, yet undaunted, the young man reached down, lifted his pants, and removed the ankle weights that he always practiced in. He picked up his ball and went back to the other side of the court. Everything looked the same on his second attempt, but he seemed a little bit faster. He exploded upward with more power, and he rose to a height no five-foot-nine-inch eighth-grader should be able to reach. The onlookers cheered enthusiastically as the young man rocked the rim with a thunderous dunk!

"Fast-forward a bit. This young man grew into a hardwood phenom. Colleges chomped at the bit to get him on their teams. He was a superstar in his neighborhood, and his future was undoubtedly headed for the NBA. Except, he never laid aside those weights holding him down. I'm not talking about those ankle weights. I mean the real weights.

You see, this young man came from a broken home. A home where violence, abuse and abandonment were as regular as the evening news. He practiced for hours because it was the only place he knew where he could find peace. To him, a crime-ridden park where bullets fly weekly was more peaceful than hearing the screaming or seeing his parents battling each other, or feeling their wrath when he was the only outlet. And those bystanders watching him were drug dealers working in their 'office,' which is what they called the park he practiced in.

"It took a spark during his first year in college to trigger the conflagration that is inevitable when we store the weights of anger, resentment, confusion and fear over and over again in our hearts. That spark was the death of his father figure, which unfortunately wasn't his actual father. This death led the young man down a self-destructive path that saw his sobriety disappear within days, his scholarship fade away within weeks, and his life bound behind iron bars within a year. Those ankle weights were nothing compared to the weights piled up on his mind, his heart and his soul.

"So, my question today is, what weights are we still carrying? What burdens are blocking the incredible, indescribable things God wants to do in our lives? What excess baggage are we still lugging around that hinders, or even prevents, us from running the race God has set before us?

"Every adult on the face of the earth is carrying some baggage. This sinful world has shown us things that we were not created to see; told us lies we were not created to hear; taught us lessons we were not created to know. Many times we can't receive more of God because we are full already. The more of this life we have lived, the more we have been filled by its damnable lies. Somewhere out there is a little boy who was violated by someone he trusted; today, he wears a suit and tie and goes to work every day carrying the scars of his tainted past. Somewhere out there is a little girl whose parents gave her tons of religion but never showed her how to have a relationship with God; today she's a respected surgeon who thinks heaven is a fairytale for the weak-minded. Somewhere out there is a teenager who never knew his dad; today he gets to chill with his homies on the yard for an hour a day. Somewhere in here is a ten-year-old boy who discovered the birds and the bees from an adult magazine; today, he's wearing a clergy collar and preaching the word of God.

"Jesus said no one can come to Him unless the Father draws them. Life fills our cups with so much pain, anger, lies, shame, despair and misinformation, it literally takes an act of God to get us to just accept His free gift of salvation! And since He loves us so much, He calls us to Himself just as we are—broken vessels and filled cups. So full that when God tries to pour more of His power, His wisdom, His presence into us, we can't receive Him, because we never made room. So full that coming to church every now and then is more than many folks can handle, and reading His word is completely out of reach. We may come to Christ for salvation, but too often we stop well short of transformation.

Why? Well, 'It is hard to fill a cup that is already full.' "

What weights are we still carrying? Yet another question that pierced Solomon to the core. Everything he had done and experienced over the past few days was encapsulated in that one terrifying question. Solomon spent his adult life trying to solve problems and fix broken things, but the word that day made him wonder, *Maybe I'm the problem. Maybe I'm the one who needs fixing. Maybe I'm the one who's broken.* There was no denying it, no dodging it. God was doing a full-court press on Solomon's heart. As he sat spellbound by the sermon that was seemingly prepared specifically for him, Grammy gently took his hand and squeezed it softly. She felt it too. And she knew her "little boy" could use the reassuring strength that only a mother could give.

After service Solomon approached Pastor Jefferson. He intended to shake his hand and compliment him on a powerful message, but, once again, the well of emotion within him changed his best-laid plans.

"Pastor, that was—," Solomon paused to clear his throat. "Your message today, it really hit—" All of a sudden, the words wouldn't come out. From out of nowhere, a boulder materialized in the back of his throat, and tears began to well. Pastor Jefferson walked forward and embraced his wayward, hurting brother. No words were spoken, but the two mighty men of God just hugged. Solomon refused to lose it like he had done all weekend, but he couldn't stop a few tears from falling. Pastor Jefferson was his friend and mentor, yet Solomon purposely pulled away from him when he left his collar on the ground. In the military, Solomon had learned that you never leave your comrade in the heat of a battle. Yet that's exactly what he did. When Solomon left his calling, he also left his comrade—his friend—uncovered on the spiritual battlefield. Sitting in the back all this time was a way for him to hide from facing his own guilt and shame for deserting Pastor Jefferson. Now, this guilt and shame refused to be bottled up anymore.

"Pastor, I am so sorry for leaving like I did. I'm so sorry I never came to you."

Pastor Jefferson responded, "I forgive you. You are and will always be my brother. The journey you are on is ordained by the Lord. The gifts and call upon your life are given by God, without repentance. Trust Him. Trust His process. And watch His miracle unfold."

15

"Again, truly I tell you that if two of you on earth agree about anything they ask for, it will be done for them by my Father in heaven. For where two or three gather in my name, there am I with them."

Matthew 18:19-20

Solomon wondered what happened to Gabby. He hadn't heard from her in a couple of weeks. He didn't see her in service the last two Sundays, and she didn't answer or return his calls. Though he had only known her for a few weeks, he felt a bond with her that he had not felt since Gloria. The girls would laugh and poke fun at their dad, calling him love-struck and smitten. (Bethany had returned to Los Angeles, so her ribbing came via cell phone.) But Solomon knew it wasn't love at first sight, though he didn't mind it leading in that direction. Gabby had been such an instrumental piece of this life turning-point that he couldn't understand why she would disappear while he was still working his way around the bend.

Solomon was chewing on Pastor Jefferson's sermon long after that Sunday. He got a recording of it to listen to, because he knew it was God speaking. He realized the apology that came pouring out of him after the pastor's sermon was a little more of the baggage he had been storing. Since that day, he felt freer to worship, freer to soar to the rafters in his praise. *I lost some of that "weight" I've been carrying.* He didn't feel ready to jump back into the clergy yet, though. He knew he needed to complete the "turn," lest he jump out deeper than his recovery could sustain. Yet, he felt the urge to minister—to serve—again. And as God would have it, Simone provided the perfect opportunity for Solomon to ease back onto that battlefield.

"Hey, Daddy," Simone beamed as she bounced downstairs.

"Hey. Why are you all dressed up?"

"Uh, I'm in jeans and a T-shirt. That hardly qualifies as 'dressed up.'"

"Well, it's more dressed up than shorts, a tank top and slippers. You headed out?"

"Daddy! It's the fourth Thursday of the month. The mission, remember?" Every fourth Thursday of the month, for the past seven months, Sherrie took Simone to the Light House Rescue Mission to serve food and pray for the homeless.

"That's right. I forgot what day it is," Solomon replied. "Well, as always, be safe and prayed up."

"I will, Daddy. It's totally safe and awesome, though. I never thought I would love hanging around with homeless people, but once I got over myself, I just see them as people now, people who could use a friendly smile, some hot food and, most of all, someone who sees them—not a beggar, not a problem, not a nuisance, but a person.

"I have friends there, and I love how they light up when we

talk. There's this one lady, Janet. She is my buddy. I go sit with her and laugh when I take a break from serving. The first day I went, I was so nervous. Everything was so . . . just weird and foreign. She could tell I was uncomfortable, so she actually came up to me and smiled. She had the gnarliest teeth I'd ever seen. I almost jumped back, which made me feel even worse, 'cause I knew I was making things worse. But Janet didn't even flinch. She kept her smile and told me I better throw away the licorice stick I was holding or else my smile would end up looking like hers. I just burst out laughing. Can you believe it? She was actually comforting me! From that moment on, I felt cool and welcomed. Janet is the best, but they're all real cool. Hey, why don't you come with us tonight?"

Every fourth Thursday of the month, Solomon had scheduled absolutely nothing—and he liked it that way. His evenings were his to relax or to tinker with some broken thing. But this request wasn't normal. Once again, he felt the Lord in it. *Why tinker with broken things when I can help mend broken vessels?*

"Sure. Call Sherrie and let her know we'll meet her there."

The Light House Mission had touched thousands of lives over the years. It began when a few idealistic undergrads decided to end hunger, one mouth at a time. Of course, college tuition doesn't leave much money for philanthropy, but they knew hunger doesn't care how it's fed, so they found the cheapest food they could—beans and corned-beef hash—and a value pack of paper plates and put their conviction into action. After graduation, they put their degrees together, got a grant and started the Light House. At first they rented an old beat-up restaurant that was barely big enough to seat eight people, but with every filled belly, God extended more grace and opened more doors. In time, the big grocery chains started to supply soon-to-be-outdated food. Churches started approaching them for opportunities to help serve. And big-pocket donors started writing checks. Eventually, the young dreamers bought an old warehouse about fifteen miles away and went from serving food to managing a life-changing organization that provided food, limited shelter, counseling, bus passes, laundromat tokens, job placement and even pro bono legal counsel—all from a few cans of beans and hash, and the heart to help those who needed it the most.

Fourth Thursday was the day Sherrie's church handled "service" at the mission. The team separated into three groups: food prep, food service and prayer warriors. Simone always worked the food service crew, while Sherrie was a stalwart prayer warrior. She had been praying for souls at the mission for the past seven years, but her connection to the Light House started years earlier, on the other side of the serving table.

Three years after she last saw Coach Stevenson, Sherrie found herself in the pigpen of her young life. The girl who was too fast on and off the track squandered a scholarship with too many nights spent partying. When she came home addicted to drugs and pregnant by a man her fundamentalist father didn't approve of, he disowned her and kicked her out of the house. So three months pregnant, unemployed, undereducated and homeless, young Sherrie ended up at the Light House. It was rock bottom, but it was the place where her new life began. The first evening at the mission, a prayer warrior approached her, but Sherrie rebuffed her, almost violently. The prayer warrior didn't blink or even hesitate. She looked Sherrie straight in the eyes and declared, "I rebuke you, unclean spirits! In the name of Jesus, leave this child of God now!"

Sherrie woke up a few minutes later, lying on a sofa in a back room, with the prayer warrior holding her hand and praying in a language she had never heard before. She didn't know what the prayer warrior was saying, but something in her told her not to speak, not to interrupt. So, she lay there for what seemed like an hour as the woman cast down spiritual strongholds and interceded for the wayward young lady.

Sherrie didn't understand why, but she felt—different. It was hard for her to describe at the time, so she would just tell people it was like a fog lifted. Sherrie spent the rest of the night talking to the prayer warrior about the Lord and salvation in a way that she never had before. She had gone to church every Sunday growing up; she had been raised to know God is God and Jesus is His Son. But there was something this prayer warrior had that Sherrie felt deep down she needed badly. The prayer warrior kept calling God "Father," and she said it with such affection, such conviction. Sherrie came across plenty of pious folks, but she had never known someone with such a personal connection with God. With the lifting of the fog, Sherrie became acutely aware of the vacuum in her heart, and every answered question only made the spotlight on that hole brighter. When the prayer warrior finally asked, "Are you ready to accept the gift of new life that Jesus, the Son of the living God, has provided?" Sherrie blubbered "Y-ye-yes" in between sobs. That night, Sherrie was reborn. Over the next six days, she sought prayer from every single prayer warrior that came to the mission, but she never saw "her" prayer warrior again.

Within two years, the Lord restored the foundations of Sherrie's life, blessing her with sobriety, a career and a child with no effects from the many poor choices she made while he lay helpless in her womb. She also immersed herself in the Word, feasting like a woman who had been starved her whole life. She joined the church that ministered to her that first night, mostly to grow in the ways of the Lord but also hoping that her angel would reappear someday. She also volunteered at the mission, graduating from food prepper to food server to prayer warrior.

"Hey, sweetie!" Sherrie greeted Simone with a smile as big as the room.

"Hey, Ms. Sherrie. You remember my daddy, Solomon?"

"Of course. So glad to see you, Pastor Solomon. We already got a few folks in, and there will be plenty more to come, so let's get to work. Pastor, I know you are just visiting, but are you able to put in a little work tonight?"

"Absolutely," Solomon beamed. It had been a long, long time since he felt called and emboldened to minister. A surge of energy and enthusiasm streaked through him as he symbolically rolled up his sleeves and said, "Let's get to work. Lead the way, ma'am."

"You can be one of our prayer warriors then."

"OK. Point me in the right direction."

Sherrie smiled at the eager Light House neophyte. "Well, not me, Pastor, the Holy Spirit. The prayer warriors mingle with the people, talk to them, and as the Holy Spirit leads, we ask them if they will let us pray for them. Sometimes we don't even ask, 'cause if the Spirit says 'get in the fight,' we don't wait for anyone else's permission. The team is waiting for us over there in the corner. We'll pray together and then fan out as the Spirit moves."

As the evening wore on, Solomon's enthusiasm never waned. He didn't approach anyone with a "let-me-help-this-poor-soul" mind-set, but rather a genuine desire to connect with real people. Listening to their stories, laughing at their jokes and telling some of his own brought a satisfaction that had been missing for some time. Indeed, Solomon ministered, but, in truth, the experience ministered to him, especially the connection he made with Staff Sergeant Kenneth Barnes.

Sgt. Barnes was a Light House regular who had served ten years in the Army. He almost always sat by himself, wearing his old Army fatigue top. He rarely gave the prayer warriors more than a couple of minutes before brushing them away with a "Well, thanks for stopping by, but this food ain't gonna eat itself." Solomon, though, as a fellow veteran, got an extended pass.

"Hooah!" Solomon said, as he walked up to the table Sgt. Barnes was sitting at.

Sgt. Barnes looked up, shocked to hear the old Army battle cry. With a mouth full of chicken, he belted back "Hooah! Sit down, brother! Name's Ken."

"Nice to meet you, Ken. I'm Solomon." Solomon reached his hand across the table. Ken, unwilling to relinquish the drumstick he was devouring, extended a chicken-clutching fist in response. The two bumped knuckles as Solomon took a seat.

"I punched in '07—four years," Solomon began.

"Did ten years. Got out in '08," Ken replied. "Did you see any action?"

"Plenty. You?"

"I did two tours in Afghanistan before I punched. Infantry."

"Rangers. After eighteen months in Iraq, I decided to trade my rifle for the Word. So, I stayed in the fight against evil; I just shifted fronts."

They both laughed at the comment. Solomon felt eerily comfortable talking to Ken. Two grizzled vets connecting in a way that's only possible between souls who have seen and done things most humans couldn't imagine.

"Man, you sound like you should've been the one briefing the UN instead of Colin Powell!" Ken laughed even more. "You ate that whole 'Axis of Evil' bullcrap right up, didn't you?"

Solomon ran into plenty of soldiers like Ken during his stint in the service. Solomon was always the idealist, always the one fighting to keep America safe, protecting his family half a world away. And he was always the butt of poster-boy jokes. He actually wore it as a badge of honor. He knew the men around him may have been there for different reasons, but he also knew they had a special brotherhood, and though a few weren't too keen to take a bullet for the Stars and Stripes, they would quickly run through a hail of gunfire to pull him out of harm's way if he went down. He missed that brotherhood and felt a hint of it again as he sat across from Ken.

"Guilty as charged," Solomon replied. "Yeah, the fellas called me Captain America."

"Well, I kinda started out that way. More pissed off than patriotic, though. The embassy bombings in Africa lit a fire under my ass—excuse me, Reverend—under my behind, and I just wanted to go kick someone's a—, uh, tail. Then, 9/11 sent me through the friggin' roof. That's probably why I re-upped for another go in the desert. I was runnin' on piss and vinegar in those days. Not a whole lot going on upstairs, just all testosterone, beer and anger. But as I kept losing more and more friends in a war that seemed less and less right, I kinda started to forget who I was supposed to be mad at."

"Is that what made you decide to call it quits?"

"Well, I didn't really have a choice in that one. Got hooked on heroin in the desert. It's amazing what you can find in the middle of a friggin' war zone, if you look hard enough. I saw a shrink, and she told me that I was trying to escape the pain of losing so many friends. Bullcrap! I just wanted to get high 'cause I was tired of being pissed all the time."

Solomon became very serious, as he felt he finally knew what he was there to pray for. "Is that what brings you here, brother?"

"Hell no! Hunger pains brought me here!" They both laughed, refusing to let the magnitude of the situation get in the way of a good joke. "Yeah, Reverend, I never did fully shake it. I get right for a while, but it just doesn't stick. Can you pray for me?"

It was the first time Ken had ever asked a prayer warrior to pray for him. Solomon, though, was unsettled by the jocular request. "Yes, I *can* pray for you, but I'd like to know what you *really* want."

"What do you mean, Rev?"

"Did you just come here to eat? Did you just come here to hang out? Did you just come to give the prayer warriors crap?"

Ken became serious for the first time that evening. Something about that question resonated. For so long, he had resigned himself to the life he was living, content that, eventually, he would just die and be done with it. But Solomon's question knocked at the door of something he had shut a long time ago— his heart. *Did I really want to just eat, get high and die?* Ken looked up at Solomon with watery eyes and answered, "I want to be free, Reverend. I don't want to wake up on the street no more. I don't want to be an addict no more. Please, pray for me, Solomon."

"Please take my hands." Solomon reached his hands across the table. Ken grabbed them, almost desperately.

"Ken, do you believe that Jesus is the Son of God?"

"Yes, sir."

"Do you believe that He died for your sins?"

"Yes, sir."

"Do you believe that He rose from the dead and is in Heaven interceding for you?"

"Yes, sir."

"Heavenly Father, with You, all things are possible. When You spoke to nothing, it obeyed and became a universe. We are so grateful to be called children of the Most High God. We look forward to the day when every knee bows and every tongue confesses that Jesus Christ is Lord. We are here, touching and agreeing, seeking your divine intervention in the life of my brother Ken. Lord, the spirit is willing, but the flesh is weak. In the name of Jesus, please set Ken free from the shackles of addiction. Please set Ken free from the anger and the pain that opened the door to addiction. Please Father, glorify your Son by restoring what this corrupt world has stolen from my brother. Give Ken a testimony of healing, deliverance and transformation that will draw others to your Son's kingdom.

"Ken, speak to your Father. Tell Him what your spirit is speaking to you right now."

Ken had started shaking. He had spent so many years laying brick after brick around his heart, and now, finally, he saw his impenetrable wall for what it truly was—a facade no stronger than Styrofoam. With a quivering voice, Ken looked up to heaven and yelled, "Help me! I'm sorry for all the wrong I've done. I don't want to be this person anymore. Please, Lord. Help me!"

Solomon hugged the smelly, dirty, heroin addict for a long time, as prayer warriors everywhere wiped away tears and praised God for another prodigal son who started the journey home. Simone looked on from behind the food table awash in joy and Godly pride for her daddy.

"Thank you, Jesus," she said softly, transfixed by the Holy Ghost-moment between the two prodigal sons.

Eventually, Ken loosened his grip. "Thank you, brother."

"No, Ken. Thank you. Thank you for having the courage and the faith to cry out to God. Your new journey starts right now. It won't be easy, but you already know what the road behind you looks like. The road ahead starts with surrendering, continues with trusting and ends with shining. Surrender your will to His, trust His work in you, and shine the light of Christ brighter and brighter as you draw closer to Him."

Ken wiped away tears from his weathered, unshaven cheeks. "Brother, I'm ready for that new start. I need it. I don't want to carry this baggage anymore. I know drugs ain't trivial, but I call it baggage. Been carryin' it since the war; it's almost like I never left the 'Stan. I'm ready to come home. Now what?"

"Well, Ken," Solomon answered, "I'm gonna walk you over to one of the coordinators. But I want to give you my phone number first. God didn't bring me here to pray and leave. I want to walk with you on your road to recovery. Let me know how I can reach you as well."

Ken looked at Solomon in disbelief and gratitude. It had been a long, long time since he truly felt he had someone in his corner. As the two men walked to the mission office, Solomon slapped his hand upon Ken's dusty shoulder like a big brother. Ken stopped abruptly, looked at Solomon and asked, "You carryin' any baggage from the desert?"

Solomon smiled and said, "Nope, thank God."

"Good for you, brother. No one comes through a war without scars. No one. And I ain't talkin' about the ones you can see." Ken raised his finger and tapped his head and his chest. "You may want to dig a little deeper, just to make sure ain't nothin' there."

There it is again. Dig deeper! Ken had no idea how poignant his advice was. Solomon's mouth almost hit the floor.

"You OK, brother? Looks like I mighta hit a nerve. I'm sorry. I used to have a filter between my brain and my mouth, but I lost it years ago. Don't pay no attention to me. Shoulda quit while I was ahead."

Solomon was still stunned by the moment. God doesn't do coincidences, so there was something He wanted Solomon to do —keep digging. The war was something Solomon never intentionally revisited in his mind. He had gone to counseling and group sessions right after he came back. He wasn't having nightmares or lashing out at folks, well, except for poor Errol. But God was clearly telling him to go deeper into that chapter of his life.

Solomon returned to the moment and stuttered, "K-K-Ken." He cleared his throat and said, "You don't have to apologize, bro. Matter of fact, would you mind praying for me?"

"Well, I ain't a pastor or nothin', but I'll give it a shot. Lord, uh, please help Solomon see what's really there. Show him anything he may have brought home and still ain't dealt with. Amen."

"Amen."

A woman's voice chimed in: "Amen." Both men turned around to see who was eavesdropping on the prayer. Gabby stood there smiling. "Hello, boys."

16

"Therefore, do not let sin reign in your mortal body, that you should obey it in its lusts. And do not present your members as instruments of unrighteousness to sin, but present yourselves to God as being alive from the dead, and your members as instruments of righteousness to God. For sin shall not have dominion over you, for you are not under law but under grace."

Romans 6:12-14

"Gabby? What are you doing here?" The words flew out of Solomon's mouth before he could think.

Gabby just smiled, taking no offense to the curt greeting. "Nice to see you, too, Solomon. Hi, Ken."

"Hey, Gabby. He's right, where you been? I've been missing that voice of yours."

Solomon stood there flabbergasted and confused. He tried to speak, but, instead of words, only incoherent grunts burped out. His mind was desperately trying to catch up to a moment that had somehow sailed by. Seeing Gabby again was nice, but seeing Gabby at the moment a perfect stranger told him to do the exact same thing she had told him to do was mind-blowing. And then for her to actually know this perfect stranger was just too much to figure out all at once, so total brain lock ensued.

"Dang, brother, you act like you never seen a pretty girl before," Ken interjected. "This li'l lady's got a voice like an angel."

"Thank you, Ken," Gabby responded. "Solomon, I sing praise and worship songs during dinner here. I've just been away for a while. I'm a little late, but it looks like the Lord got me here right on time!"

Look at God! Solomon thought. His heaven-sent muse showed up at the perfect time to guide him through yet another round of spiritual, emotional and psychological excavation.

"Praise God for you, Ken!" Gabby hugged Ken but gave a wry smile to Solomon, as if to say, "It ain't all about you."

Solomon could only laugh at his selfish assessment of the situation. How soon he forgot a wayward soul just cried out to God for help. He nodded his head and shrugged his shoulders, as if to say, "True. So true."

The hug lasted a little longer than one would expect between two relative strangers. Even Ken, who hadn't enjoyed the embrace of a woman in quite some time, started to feel a bit awkward. Yet, he couldn't let go. As gravity glues your feet to the floor, an unknown force fastened him to Gabby. Every part of his dusty body that touched her felt warm. The feeling didn't just hover at the surface; Ken felt it soaking into himself ever so slowly. His brain screamed, *Let the woman go before she calls the cops*, but the rest of him refused to listen.

Eventually, Gabby whispered, "Ken, if the Son sets you free, you will be free indeed. Go and be who you were created to be."

She released the repentant vagabond as a tear crept down his leathery face. Solomon touched Ken's shoulder to lead him to the Light House coordinators. As the two men walked away, Solomon turned to Gabby and said, "Now, don't disappear on me, OK?"

Gabby smiled and replied, "I can't make any promises. I'm a busy girl."

When Solomon returned, Simone stood there beaming. An impossibly wide smile and open arms greeted him. It had been a long, long time since Simone had felt this feeling. For so long, it seemed, she had looked at Solomon as if *he* were the victim of that distant attack. His forlorn, sullen demeanor left her, most of the time, feeling sorry for the man she was supposed to revere. But now she had that "daddy's little girl" feeling again—immense pride in the first hero she had ever known.

"Man, that was incredible, Daddy!" she said as she almost jumped into his arms.

"Yeah, that was pretty special. Thank you for inviting me tonight. You have no idea how good it feels to be back in the fight, to make a difference."

"I'll bet! Nobody gets more than thirty seconds with Mr. Ken, and you got fifteen minutes and his soul!" Simone bragged.

"Honey, remember, he's the fish, and we are just the bait; the Holy Spirit is the one doing the fishing."

"I know, I know, but let a girl marinate in this for a bit. God will be OK if I pop your collar. *You* just can't pop your collar." They both laughed off the playful comment.

Gabby had taken the microphone and was now singing "How Great Thou Art." Her voice resonated through his ears down into his soul. Each note had such perfect pitch; each word came from such a deep place of adoration that even the deaf couldn't help but be affected. And Solomon looked at the glowing soprano with such a serene longing, Simone couldn't help but notice.

"Daddy, you OK?"

"Yes, honey. She just has such an amazing voice. I almost forgot."

"I could introduce you before we leave. Wait. You know Ms. Gabby?"

"Yes, I do. Remember the lady I mentioned to you? The one who's been helping me deal with some things? Well, there she is."

"No way! She's the Gabby you were talking about? Gabby is soooo cool. She's been singing here for like three months. What a small world."

"Ain't that the truth. We gotta get back to work. People need to eat, and souls need prayer."

"Right. Love you, Daddy."

"Love you too."

Gabby sang for the rest of the evening. Solomon spoke with and prayed for a few more people, with each encounter pouring a little more honey on his soul. As the evening came to a close, the three came together near the serving tables. Simone had been on her feet serving for over an hour, Gabby had been singing for the last thirty minutes, and Solomon had completed a meandering 5K, going from table to table as the Spirit led. The volunteers always ate last at the Light House, so the three sat down to enjoy a nice meal together and bask in the afterglow of a wonderful night.

Simone told them how three different people came through the line for seconds, but each had totally different assessments of the food. "That's the best meatloaf I ever had!" "I came back to get some more meatloaf; it's harder than a brick, so I might as well throw it at the next driver that won't roll their window down!" "Do you mind if I get another plate of meatloaf? I got a friend who couldn't make it tonight."

Solomon asked her, "Was it hard for you to serve folks when they didn't appreciate it?"

"Well, when I first started serving, I did get in my feelings a little. But now I'm good."

The uber-athlete was inhaling her food. Standing on her feet serving food for what seemed like forever made her surprisingly hungry. Plus, she had school in the morning, so there was never much time at the end of the night to waste. Sherrie would usually help close things up and, within fifteen minutes of Simone starting her meal, would come to take her home. And, like clockwork, Sherrie sauntered over.

"Hey, family!"

"Hey, Ms. Sherrie. I'll be done in a second."

"Honey, your dad's here, remember? Don't think you'll be needin' a ride from me tonight. I just came by to love on y'all before I go." Sherrie flung her arms open, and Simone gleefully accepted the embrace and then sat back down to the few bites left of her meal.

Sherrie turned to Gabby and said, "Girl, that voice of yours is heaven-sent. I was a little worried you wouldn't make it tonight. You sure have a gift to just usher in the presence of the Lord."

"Thank you so much, Sherrie. To God be the glory."

"Pastor," Sherrie said, turning to Solomon, "what God did through you tonight was so powerful. I have seen Ken in here forever, and every time you could just see the weight on him, even though he always tried to hide it under that gruff exterior. We've been interceding for him for so long, and to see God get the increase tonight literally made me cry. I praise God for you, Pastor." Sherrie warmly wrapped her arms around Solomon, and as she released him, she said, "Before I leave y'all to your evening, I'm curious to know what the Lord did to open his heart to you."

"Well, the bond between soldiers is strong, and the bond between war vets is even stronger."

"Ah, look at God. He got you up off the sofa to help Ken finish the journey home. Thank you so much for answering His call tonight. I'll be praisin' all the way home!"

"Truth be told, Sherrie, God used Ken just as much as He used me. Actually, I was wondering if you wouldn't mind giving Simone a ride home?"

Sherrie gave the newly (re)minted prayer warrior a double take. *Is this man of God really pawning his daughter off on me so he can spend some one-on-one time with Gabby?* Her warm smile evaporated.

"That would be great!" Simone proclaimed. "I did want to talk to you, Ms. Sherrie, about some private girl stuff, so that would be perfect!"

While the look on Sherrie's face was one part astonishment, two parts mortification, and a thousand parts righteous indignation, Simone was positively beaming. The thought of her daddy finally jumping off the sideline and getting back in the game was just too good to let slip away. And if all it took was a little white lie to make it happen, she was more than happy to oblige.

Solomon would have had to be deaf, mute, blind and otherwise dead to miss either the daggers emanating from Sherrie's icy gaze or Simone's exuberant attempts to clear the runway for him.

"Pump your brakes, Simone. It's not what either of you think. Ken said something to me, and I know it was the Holy Spirit talking. I had no idea Gabby would be here tonight, but she showed up at exactly the right moment. God doesn't do coincidences, so I would really like to talk to Gabby about what I think He wants me to share with her. Sherrie, I would not normally do this, but as you said, God got me up off my sofa for a reason—well, reasons. There's still some more He wants to accomplish with me, and I believe Gabby is a part of His plan for me tonight."

Solomon's measured words helped to soften Sherrie's demeanor. "Alright, Pastor. I'll be happy to." As the two women walked arm in arm to the door, Simone turned and gave her dad a big smile and a little wink. *In one ear, out the other,* Solomon thought, as he just smiled and sat back down.

Curiously, Gabby had said nothing at all during the whole somewhat tense exchange. She just sat there observing the verbal dance. "That Sherrie is something else. Such a good heart, and so much passion. I thought she was about to go completely berserk on you for a minute there."

"Yeah, I knew I had to clean that up real quick. I probably still got some cleaning up to do on that one. I just hope she's not the rumor-spreading kind."

"I think you're safe. So, what did you want to talk about?"

"Well, first, thank you for taking the time to listen. You remember when you arrived, Ken was praying for me?"

"Yes. He asked the Lord to open your eyes, right?"

"Right. Ken and I connected because we both served in combat. Ken said something that made my jaw drop to the floor.

He said nobody gets through a war without scars. I already knew that, and had the therapy to prove it. But then he said I need to keep digging. When he said that, I just about fell over. I know the Holy Spirit said that through him, because it's exactly what He said through you. And then two seconds later, you showed up out of the blue. So, I believe there is something I need to share with you."

Gabby sat still. She was also taken aback by the serendipitous chain of events Solomon was describing. The Lord had not clued her into anything different about her work in the vineyard that night. It would appear a simple night of singing to God's glory would not be so simple after all.

Unbeknownst to anyone, Gabby's day had been anything but pleasant. Her venerable horseless carriage decided to take an extended nap in the middle of traffic, forcing her to wait nearly an hour for a tow truck to arrive. Meanwhile, a rather clueless driver chose that exact moment to demonstrate his complete lack of driving prowess by plowing into the back of Gabby's broken vehicle. By the time the tow truck arrived, and everything got sorted out, she found herself at the mechanic's, four hours after her journey began—having completed zero errands—and six hours after her most recent meal.

Having a broken down, mangled car can take 'hangriness' to an entirely new level, even for the saintliest Christian. Gabby found herself getting snippy with the incompetent driver, the tow truck driver, the insurance agent and the mechanic—and only one of the four actually "deserved" it. Thank God the auto body shop occupied the same corner as a Chinese fast-food restaurant and a bus stop. Gabby sat there eating the most questionable meal she had had in a long, long time as if it were a Gordon Ramsey culinary creation; hunger will lower even the loftiest standards. And seeing that time was far spent, she chose to take the bus directly to the Light House Mission, since home was in the opposite direction. Gabby needed some praise and worship just as much as the poor souls she would be singing to.

"I'm all ears, Solomon, but I don't think the Light House will stay open long enough for me to hear it. Funny thing is, I could use a ride home. I'm about thirty minutes away. Wanna tell me on the way?"

"Deal."

17

"Then Jacob was left alone; and a man wrestled with him until the breaking of day . . . And he said, 'Let me go, for the day breaks.' But he said, 'I will not let you go unless you bless me!'"

Genesis 32:24-26

The night sky and a cool breeze greeted them as they left the mission. Solomon had parked about a block away. Gabby felt the chill immediately. Her noon-day sweater was proving to be totally insufficient for the nighttime temperature. She pulled the collar of her sweater up as far as it could go and folded her arms tight across her chest. Seeing her obvious discomfort, Solomon reached his arm over her shoulder and pulled her close.

"My car is just up the block. We'll get you warm in a jiffy."

"Thank you," Gabby responded, through clenched teeth.

As they walked on, a car passed in the opposite direction. It was moving unusually slow. As it got closer, Solomon recognized the incredibly shocked and almost ecstatic face of his little girl, Simone, in the passenger seat. Her hand covered her mouth, as if to muffle the scream emanating from her exuberant heart.

Solomon couldn't stop the small smile that spontaneously appeared. But then he remembered who was driving. If there was ever such a thing as a "death stare", Sherrie had perfected it in that moment. As the car crept past, Sherrie slowly turned her head to maintain her angry, laser-lock glare.

Oh boy! Solomon knew he had some explaining to do to ensure his good did not become evil spoken of. Gabby didn't notice a thing, her chin burrowed into her neck and her eyes focused on each step it took to get her to warmth.

After a brisk walk, Solomon and Gabby arrived. The gentleman preacher opened her door and helped the diminutive lady up to her seat in his big, manly truck. He hurried to the driver's side to turn on the engine and get the warm air flowing.

"It'll get warm pretty quick," Solomon said. "You're a little underdressed for this time of year."

"Well, the day didn't go quite like I expected," Gabby responded.

Solomon could sense Gabby was monumentally understating things. "Gabby, we all have days we wish didn't happen. But I am so impressed and inspired that, in spite of whatever happened today, you pressed your way to serve others—and knowing you would be out in the cold, without a sure ride home! You're an amazing woman and an example of what we all should aspire to."

Gabby smiled. His kind words helped warm her even more than the heater. "Well, the bus stops right across the street from the mission and my apartment, so it's not like I planned on walking five miles uphill, in the snow, both ways. But thank you. I appreciate it, and the ride. It certainly has been a terrible day, but, by God's grace, I'm still here. I have to make a few phone calls tomorrow to apologize to four different people, though. Well, three different people, but that's another story. I pressed my way here for more than praise and worship, just like you gave up a night of doing whatever it was you were doing for more than Ken's deliverance. So, what's on your mind?"

As Solomon pulled out from the curb, he took a deep breath and then began. "I saw some terrible things in Iraq; I did some terrible things in Iraq. I was an Army Ranger, so we were never too far from the fight. I had a lot of friends who didn't make it out alive or in one piece. Seeing the things I saw will mess anyone up in the head. And the hardest thing about war is seeing those things happen to the men you racked with for thirteen months, men you've shed blood for, men you've grown to become more than friends with. They become your brothers. You may not even like most of them, but you love 'em because they are the ones that help you keep going. You love the letters you get from back home because they help you keep your humanity. You treasure the occasional phone call with your family. But it's the soldiers fighting with you that help you keep a hold on your sanity, because in the silence, all you have are your brothers."

"I'm sorry to interrupt, but what do you mean 'the silence'?"

"That's alright, Gabby. The silence is kinda hard to explain, but every combat veteran knows it. It's that place in the heat of the fight when bullets are bouncing off walls and helmets, when soldiers are screaming orders or cuss words or just plain screaming. A mortar round goes off nearby and just knocks you for a loop. You're lying there on the ground, dirt all over you, and you hear—nothing. The bullets are still flying, bombs are still going off, but you hear nothing. Your head is all loopy from the concussion, and you're trying to figure out whether you're alive or dead, injured or whole, conscious or out cold. That's the silence. At that moment, you might think of your wife or kids or your girl back home. But none of them can help you. Then, you look and see your brother rushing over to cover you. And you look to your left and see another brother kneeling over you. His mouth is moving, but you still don't hear anything. Then he checks you over and pats you on the shoulder and helps you back up and into the fight. That's the silence. No one can meet you in your silence except the soldier who's right there with you."

"Oh." Gabby sat stunned by the vivid image Solomon had painted. "My God, my God. Thank you for explaining. I will never forget what the silence is."

Solomon smiled weakly. His war days were always a difficult subject for him to discuss, especially in detail. It always dug up emotions that he had dealt with and buried ages ago.

"Neither will I, Gabby. There was this one time just outside Mosul. We were doing some reconnaissance near a suspected insurgent base of operations. There were about eight of us that day. We climbed this really rugged ridge to try and come up behind their position. We were only supposed to locate and report, because our unit was too small to win any significant firefight. Well, war never works out exactly as you plan. As I was coming down the ridge, I slipped and fell a couple feet. I got a few scrapes, but the problem was I sent a bunch of rocks and debris down the ridge, which gave away our position. The Ali Babas brought the thunder."

"The what? What's an Ali Baba?"

"Sorry. The insurgents brought the thunder. They fired

everything up into those rocks, including the RPG that took 50 percent of the hearing in my right ear. RPG stands for rocket-propelled grenade." Gabby smiled, appreciative that Solomon saved her from having to interrupt him again. "The explosion felt like it was as close as you are to me now. It knocked me a few feet sideways. I laid there on that ridge in the silence. I don't know how long I was laying there. Seconds feel like minutes in the silence. Eventually, one of my brothers met me in my silence. In the middle of a firefight that we would almost certainly lose. He was this loudmouth private that I didn't even like, and I'm pretty sure he didn't like me, either, but there he was, kneeling over me, covering me, helping in the silence. We would have died that day if it wasn't for a drone that just happened to be close enough to rain a couple missiles down on the insurgents. The brother who met me in my silence was Cam Johnson." Solomon paused and tried to clear his throat. The next words formed a virtual dam in his mouth, refusing to move or let anything else out. "Four months later, I shot and killed him."

Gabby gasped. "Sweet Jesus." She reached over to hold Solomon's hand. She wanted to hit him with a barrage of questions. *Why? Did he attack you? Am I riding in a car with a murderer?* But she kept quiet. This was not what her friend needed right now. As Solomon choked back tears, Gabby sat quietly holding his hand and helping him cry. It wasn't a torrent like before, but a grown manly man shedding a tear behind the wheel of his big manly truck still warranted sincere empathy. The two sat silently for a while until Solomon was ready to continue.

"We got ambushed in Fallujah. Bullets were coming from everywhere. We got separated. I engaged an insurgent in a window, then wheeled around to take out what I thought was another Ali Baba coming up the alley. There was so much smoke and dust and bullets in the air, and I was all jacked up on adrenaline. I shot Johnson in the chest. He didn't make it."

Gabby's eyes started to water. "You've been holding on to this all these years?"

"It still hurts, and it always will hurt, but, no, I haven't been holding on to it. I mean, I went through emotional and mental hell for about six months afterward. I saw the chaplain on a daily basis for a while; then I practically rented space on a therapist's couch when I got back home. I even got in touch with Johnson's parents. That was one of the toughest things I've ever done, but they not only forgave me, they actually comforted me! We reach out to each other from time to time, though I haven't contacted them since before Simone's whole ordeal. "

Gabby didn't know what to say. She was sure that the issue was Solomon's unresolved remorse and guilt over that terrible mistake, but he had put in so much emotional and mental work that it didn't seem to be a weight for him. He did cry, but who wouldn't when they've dug up such a heart-wrenching episode? And those tears weren't the downpour he had when discussing Gloria and Simone. She couldn't figure out why the Holy Spirit would be silent at a moment like this. She sat there looking through the windshield, struggling to figure out what to say to the man who put his reputation on the line to confide in her.

Solomon could sense her struggle to figure out what to say. "You don't have to say anything, Gabby. I'm not searching or desperate for guidance like before. I don't know why God wanted me to tell you all that. Who knows, maybe it was for you, not me."

And there He is! she thought. Somewhere along the way, Gabby stopped listening with her spiritual ears and started to digest the whole story like a tabloid reader. It was so riveting, so exciting, so heartbreaking. She was totally enthralled. But the Lord didn't have her in that car to end her crappy day with an awesome drama. Though she pressed her way to the mission for her assignment to praise and worship Him, she found herself tired, cold and mentally spent from the day's events. In other words, she was all in her flesh. *My Lord, I didn't even pray before or during Solomon's whole story! Solomon's story wasn't for me. It's for God to minister through me!*

"No, Solomon, it wasn't for me; well, it wasn't just for me. I need to ask your forgiveness. I listened to your story. It was spellbinding. But I did so with my flesh. That's why it was so spellbinding. I checked out spiritually the minute I hit that cold air. Will you please forgive me?"

"Of course, Gabby."

"Thank you, Solomon. Now please be patient while I seek the Lord to hear what He has to say in all this." Gabby closed her eyes, released Solomon's hand and began to pray. *Father, I am sorry for shutting you out. When I came to the mission, I came needing to be emotionally rescued, and praising you lifted my spirit up. But I failed to seek your face in this. I repent. Lord, use me for your glory. Guide my mind and word my mouth."* Gabby sat for a little while longer, neither speaking nor praying, just listening, waiting for the Spirit to give her what to say.

"Solomon," Gabby began, "I recounted your whole story to the Lord. As I did, I realized what would have been obvious to me had I been tuned in from the start. I never heard you mention the Lord at all. Where was He in all that you went through? I mean, I know *where* He was, but what I mean is, where did you experience Him, seek Him, rely on Him in the midst of it?"

"Oh, he was always right there with me. I prayed before, during and after every single battle—especially during. My relationship with the Lord was seeded as a child but was forged in the fires of combat. In fact, God told me to be a preacher in the middle of a battle."

"Really?" Gabby asked. "Which battle?"

"The one I just mentioned," Solomon answered. "The one where I lost Cam."

"Oh my. So you were called after he passed?"

"Well, not really. After I shot him, I was praying God would not let him die. I was praying probably harder than I was fighting. I was kneeling in front of him, covering him and praying, and then I heard the Lord tell me this wasn't the kind of war I was meant to fight. He said His word was my weapon."

"Wow! That's a heck of a time to be called."

"You're tellin' me. Once I got back to the world and processed my grief, I did what He told me to do. I traded my stripes for a clergy collar."

"So you obeyed the call in the midst of dealing with God saying 'no' to your most fervent prayer. Do you think God should have saved Private Johnson?"

Here we go, Solomon thought. He had never been asked that question. The chaplain helped him deal with his grief. The counselor focused on his guilt. But no one ever asked *that* question.

"Of course I do," Solomon replied. "But He's in charge, not me."

"Is He?"

Solomon was blindsided by the question. He turned and looked at Gabby and was shocked to see a look of sincere inquiry. "What do you mean?"

"Remember what the Holy Spirit said at the restaurant? 'You're still bound in chains—chains that were probably forged long before Tim Stevenson showed up.' And remember what He told you at the cemetery? 'No man can be all things to someone, except the Son of Man. You built a beautiful house on sand, Solomon, and when the earth shook, your house cracked. And when it shook again, your house crumbled.' The 'house' He was referring to isn't your family; it's your walk with God."

"I don't understand," Solomon said.

"When Simone was assaulted, you felt like you failed in protecting your family. When Gloria passed, you felt like you failed her. How did you feel when Private Johnson passed?"

Solomon thought about the question to make sure he didn't just answer out of emotion. "I felt incredibly guilty for killing an innocent man."

"And when you accepted the call in the very same moment, do you think you may have brought that guilt into your new relationship? Into your calling?"

Solomon answered, "Yes, I did. It made me determined to be a better soldier for Christ than I was for my country. It made me determined to study and pray and work hard so that I would never lose a soul the way I lost Cam."

"It's a beautiful thing to be determined, to be driven to serve God in excellence. But it is a perfect thing to be surrendered to God. Surrendering to God means having complete trust in His will. It means recognizing that the journey is not yours to take, but His to lead you on. When Private Johnson passed, you pursued God with righteous abandon, and that is wonderful. But did you truly surrender to Him? It's pretty hard to completely surrender to Him if you don't fully trust Him. He let your friend—your brother —die by your hand, on the ground beside you, despite your prayers. And in the midst of it all, He chose that moment of suffering to call you into His service. Don't be honest with me, Solomon. Be honest with yourself. Be honest with Him."

At that moment, Solomon pulled up to Gabby's apartment.

"There's a little more digging you need to do," Gabby continued. "But you're almost there. The rest of your journey you must take on your own. Well, not alone, the Holy Spirit wants to take it with you, one on one. Thank you for the ride, Solomon, and for sharing something so deeply personal tonight. You are an awesome man of God. I am so excited for what He has in store for you and your precious family. All things work together for good to them that love Him and are the called according to His purpose. The best is truly yet to come." Gabby leaned over to give Solomon a hug. Solomon hadn't said much in a while. There was just so much his brain was trying to process. *No more hand-holding,* he thought. *Lord, please fill in the blanks for me.*

There was a finality in Gabby's farewell that made it clear they had reached more than their destination that night; they had reached the end of their time together. In less than a month, Gabby had impacted Solomon's life more deeply than he could have imagined. Maybe it was that same imagination that envisioned an even deeper, lasting relationship, but his spirit was in agreement. Her assignment was complete. Solomon stepped out of the truck to help Gabby climb down from her seat. The two embraced. "Good night, Gabby. Thank you. Thank you so much. May God replenish you and bless everything you put your hands to. I promise you I'll keep digging until He says I'm done."

The whole ride home, Solomon ruminated on Gabby's words. He thought about how he felt as he saw the life slipping away from Cam. He thought about how he felt as he sat having an impromptu dinner with Cam's parents eight months after killing their son. He thought about how he felt when he prayed for Gloria. He thought about how he felt when Tim Stevenson had the audacity to flirt with his daughter. He thought and thought and thought. Then he came back to Gabby's question, "Is He?" *Is God in charge? How can He not be? I left the military for Him. I joined the clergy for Him. I spend time in prayer with him. Well, I used to, and will start again.*

When Solomon arrived home, he didn't have any answers or revelations, just questions and thoughts. Simone, wearing her pajamas, greeted him with a big hug as he walked through the door. It was clear she didn't stay up just to say good-night. The anticipatory smile on her face let Solomon know he wasn't getting too far without giving her *something.*

"Honey, it's not what you're thinking. Gabby's car broke down today, and she needed a ride home. And since the mission was closing soon, I talked to her as I drove her home."

Simone's hunger for details wouldn't be satiated so easily. "Sooooo, what did you talk about?"

"I promise you, I will tell you and the whole family when the time comes. Right now, I'm honestly still trying to wrap my head around everything we talked about. I'm gonna sleep on it myself, so let's go upstairs."

Simone finally relented and walked, arm in arm, with her daddy to the stairs, but Solomon stopped just at the base. To his right, he saw the door of The Lord's Room. *"The Holy Spirit wants to take it with you, one on one."* This wasn't the time to go to bed. Solomon needed to finish digging.

"Simone, I need to sort some things out tonight. You go on up to bed."

"OK, Daddy."

Solomon kissed his little girl goodnight and headed to The Lord's Room. He closed the door softly, knelt on his comfy pillow and began to pray:

Lord, hallowed be Your great name. Your kingdom come and Your will be done on earth just as it is in heaven. Thank You for who You are and all You have already done. Lord, I am so grateful for your grace toward me. Even now, I know that you are not just calling me to you, you are running to meet me along the way. I am here, Father. You said my walk with You is founded on sand, but I don't know how. I accepted your call. I didn't do it reluctantly or dubiously. I did let go of the plow, and for that I am so, so sorry. Is that what you mean, Lord? I open my heart to your wisdom. Please help me see. Help me understand.

Solomon knelt in silence—both his mind and his mouth—waiting, listening. From time to time, he would get his Bible, flip to a certain passage and begin to read, and then go back to silent meditation on his knees. He did this for hours and hours. This was his night to wrestle with God, and he wasn't about to let go until He blessed him.

18

"Therefore, if you are offering your gift at the altar and there remember that your brother or sister has something against you, leave your gift there in front of the altar. First go and be reconciled to them; then come and offer your gift."

Matthew 5:23-24

The dawn found Solomon lying on the floor of The Lord's Room, his head resting on his thick study Bible. At some point, he had passed out from fatigue. *The spirit is willing, but the flesh is weak,* he thought, as the rays of sunlight assaulted his bleary eyes. Solomon placed his Bible back on the desk and left the room. He shuffled to the phone to call in "sick." Twenty years ago, Solomon could've put in a full day's work on a couple of hours of sleep. Not today. Before heading up to bed, he stopped by his mother's room. He knocked on the door, hard enough to get her attention if she was awake, but soft enough not to disturb her slumber if she was still asleep.

"Come on in," Grammy said, inviting him in.

Solomon opened the door to find Grammy sitting in her

seemingly centuries-old upholstered wingback chair in the corner of her room, watching the sunrise.

"Why are you up so early, Mama?"

"Honey, at my age, I don't have too many more sunrises left. No need to sleep through them now. Besides, you have The Lord's Room; I have my chair. The Lord meets us where we are, and I want to do it right here."

"When did you start doing that?" Solomon asked.

"When I moved in with you."

"Really, how come you never told me?"

"It was none of your business," Grammy replied with a sassy little roll of her neck and a playful grin. "This was my time with Him."

Solomon smiled broadly. He loved how his mother was still so "saucy," as she called it. "OK, Mama. I'm sorry to interrupt you this morning. I didn't get much rest last night, so I'm gonna take the day off and hopefully catch up on some sleep. Can you let Simone know?"

"Alright. Come on in and sit with me for a little bit." Grammy moved her feet from the ottoman and patted it with her hand as she smiled. Solomon understood that this invitation was not something he could refuse, so he shuffled in and took his seat.

"Son," Grammy began, "when you came back from the war, I was just beside myself. I couldn't thank God enough for bringing my baby back home safe and sound. And then you told me you was gonna be a preacher! Well, I couldn't have been happier or prouder. Your daddy said, 'That boy is gonna be a fighter when he grows up. Can't say what kinda fight, but he'll be throwing punches at somebody.' Never knew he was a prophet. You *are* a fighter, Solomon. You fought for this country; you fought for your family; you fought for the Lord. You're still fighting, son. Jesus said the enemy comes only to steal, and to kill, and to destroy. That's exactly what he's been trying to do to you. He thought he won last year when he got you to leave the ministry. He thought he could put another notch in his belt. But he was wrong! You are stronger than any lie he throws at you or mountain he sets in front of you or whip he uses to beat you. 'Cause God is with you, Solomon. He's with you! The enemy hasn't taken anything from you that God won't restore, and then some. Just keep fightin' the good fight of faith, Solomon. Keep fightin.' "

Grammy's words lifted Solomon. In that moment, he wasn't Solomon the preacher, or Solomon the father. He was a little boy being comforted and empowered by a loving mother. He said nothing, but the look on his face spoke louder than his words could. It was a silent communication between mother and son that was forged in the womb, where words didn't matter. Solomon leaned forward onto his knees and rested his head on his mother's chest, as she wrapped her arms around him and hugged him tightly. She held her son silently for a long time. Solomon's eyes were closed but he wasn't sleeping. He just wanted to soak up all the love and affection he could.

Eventually, Grammy relaxed her therapeutic grip, and Solomon sat back on the ottoman. "Now, what's kept you up all night?" she pivoted.

"Well, Mama, remember that lady I told you and the girls about? The woman who's been helping me dig myself out of the funk I've been in?"

"Yes, I remember," Grammy answered, with a Cheshire cat grin.

"Simone told me you spent some time together last night."

Solomon couldn't help but laugh at what Grammy was insinuating. "Yes, we did, but not in the way Simone hopes. Last night was another God incidence. Remember Cameron Johnson?"

"Of course I do," Grammy answered.

"As I drove her home, I told her about Cam. She asked if I had brought that guilt into my new walk with God. I told her it motivated me to be a better soldier for Christ, because I never wanted to lose a soul the way I lost Cam. She said my walk with God was built on sand and that surrendering to God means having complete trust in His will. I don't understand how turning a tragedy into the motivation to serve God is wrong. To me, that's turning lemons into lemonade. But I trust this lady's discernment —I know she hears from God. So I've been up all night asking God to help me understand. The revelation hasn't come yet."

Grammy's whole face lit up. She sat forward in her seat and grabbed Solomon's hands. "Sweet Jesus! God has heard your prayers. I didn't know why at the time, but He got me up this morning a little bit earlier than normal. He had me look at two scriptures. The first came in my daily devotional. It's Isaiah 26:3: 'Thou wilt keep him in perfect peace, whose mind is stayed on thee: because he trusteth in Thee.' Then, when I was praying, He had me open my Bible and read Psalm 37. What kept ringing in my head was verses 5 and 6: 'Commit thy way unto the Lord; trust also in Him; and He shall bring it to pass.' I thought God was tellin' me to trust Him more, but now I know that word is for you!"

Solomon sat up alert, quickened from his bleary-eyed haze, anxious to hear the hand-delivered message he had tarried all night for.

"Lord," Grammy continued, "help me get this out. Please give me the words. Solomon, you didn't 'lose' Cam. God is in control. When Cam died, you took guilt into a life based on freedom from guilt; then you used that guilt to drive your life. The Lord said, '*He shall bring it to pass*,' not you. It's not up to you who lives or dies. It's not up to you who comes to Christ, grows in Christ, stays in Christ or falls away from Christ. You can read the Bible from cover to cover every day, and preach a sermon so powerful that angels appear and shout 'Hallelujah,' but it won't guarantee everybody in the pews will make it to heaven."

"I know, Mama," Solomon interrupted. "I don't expect every soul I reach to heed the word."

"Yes, but you do expect to reach every soul. I see that so clearly now. I always thought it was you being zealous for God, but now I realize where it's coming from: guilt and fear. Guilt over a terrible mistake, and fear that He might make another decision that you don't agree with. Your walk with God was never rooted in complete trust in Him, trust that His will is perfect and true, no matter how much we may not agree with it. And you can't surrender to God completely if you don't trust Him completely.

"The verse from Isaiah kinda sums it all up. From the day you went into ministry, I don't know if you ever had perfect peace. How can you, if every soul you see is another chance to atone for the life you took? That's not how Jesus wants us to serve Him. That's not how He wants His children to live. Terrible things happen in war, son. I'm not gonna sit here and tell you I know why God allowed Cam to die. But He did, and He has forgiven you. Cam's parents have forgiven you. You are free, Solomon.

Don't carry that guilt anymore. You can't let fear keep you from trusting Him. It's time for you to surrender, completely, and let God be God."

It never occurred to Solomon that he hadn't fully surrendered to God. He gave up his military dreams to answer God's call, so that right there was an act of surrender. But it was no coincidence that both Grammy and Gabby said the same thing. Solomon needed to chew on this one for a while. He knew in his heart that everything Grammy said was true, but some things just need to percolate for a bit. "Thank you, Mama." With that, he stood, kissed his Mama on the forehead and walked out of the room. As he closed the door, he glanced back toward Grammy and found her hands clasped, eyes closed and head bowed.

Five hours later, Solomon awoke to the irritatingly loud sound of a garbage truck backing up. He could have slept for at least another hour, but with the slow whine of the hydraulic lifts, the loud clanging of metal hitting metal and the late-morning sun shining through the window, there was no way he could return to the wonderful REM sleep he had been enjoying. Besides, why sleep away a day off? Solomon rolled out of bed, stretched loudly, then headed off to shower the haze away. There was so much still jostling in his mind from the conversation with Grammy, his house was too small to grapple with it all, so he decided to throw on some clothes, grab a foot-long hoagie and sit at the park nearby.

The park was absolutely perfect. Since it was midday Friday, there weren't too many people milling around. The weather was neither hot nor cold, with just enough breeze to rustle the trees in that oh-so-therapeutic harmony of leaves brushing one another. And since the park was at least a dozen miles in the opposite direction of his job, Solomon didn't have to worry about a co-worker strolling by on their lunch break.

Solomon found a bench in the middle of the park and sat down. As minutes turned into an hour, his body barely moved, but his mind was racing. Grammy helped him see his ministry was founded on a lack of trust in God, a rotting seed sown by the loss of a brother in arms. But the Holy Spirit wanted him to open the aperture more, to see the panoramic photo rather than the snapshot. The past few weeks of revelation, prayer and introspection led Solomon to an inescapable reality: mistrust in God didn't just taint his ministry, it tainted his life. Gabby showed him that his marriage was corrupted by an unrealistic expectation of who he should be as a husband. That expectation put him in the impossible position of trying to be who Jesus already was. Only someone who, at best, didn't trust the Lord, or, at worst, didn't know the Lord, would try to replace the Lord. Seeing his Glo-worm suffer and die stoked the flames of mistrust in God sown that day in Iraq. Yet again he lost someone tragically, someone he couldn't save no matter how hard he tried, no matter how hard he prayed. And when God allowed his baby girl to be assaulted, that putrid kernel of mistrust sprouted into full-grown rebellion, allowing anger and unforgiveness to set up residence in his heart.

Solomon had dug to the core and could see the blotches that stained God's masterpiece over the last decade. No more digging; it was time to start climbing. In total disregard to what any random passerby might think, he fell to his knees, clasped his hands together and began to pray. "Lord, thank You for opening my eyes. Thank You for giving me understanding. I am so sorry.

Please forgive me for not trusting You. Please forgive me for having the audacity to try and wear Your shoes. Please forgive me for letting Your calling go. Please forgive me for hardening my heart toward You. Father, I beg You to create in me a clean heart and renew a right spirit in me. Lord, I surrender *all* to You. I trust You. I trust Your plan, Your ways and Your decrees. As the man asked You to help his unbelief, please help me trust You. Help me surrender to You. I want to enjoy the freedom You provided, the freedom I never truly enjoyed because of the guilt I just couldn't let go. I let it go now and forever in Jesus' name. I believe Your word, Father. All things work together for good to those who love You and are the called according to Your purpose. Your plans for me are greater than I can fathom. I yield to them and trust that what has happened and what will happen shall be for my good, no matter how difficult it might be in the moment. Now Lord, lead me. Guide me. Use me for Your glory. Show me what You want me to do next, and I shall obey. I surrender, Lord. Amen." Solomon had no more to say, but he wasn't ready to leave his penitent time before the Lord, so he continued there, silently letting his heart cry out to God.

Eventually, Solomon sat back down on the park bench. He didn't know what his next steps should be, and he realized that's exactly where he needed to be. For so long he always had to have a plan. He thought it was just him being organized and thorough in his pursuit of excellence in God, but now he recognized that need to know what to do next was yet another symptom of his lack of trust in God. This time, he would just trust God to show him the way he should take. So he continued to sit, enjoying his half-eaten hoagie, and basking in the peace of God.

He looked across the park and saw a young couple walking together. Their arms were wrapped around each other, and they were laughing as they strolled. *They must be starting their weekend early*, Solomon thought. The movie theater was on the other side of the park, so they were probably going to catch a matinee. But as they got a little closer, Solomon's eyes grew wide. He recognized that young man. It was Errol, the guy he assaulted on Family Movie Night! At first Solomon reacted like a protective—and judgmental—dad: *I knew it! Just a little playboy. Hugged up on some other girl just a month after trying to be hugged up on my little girl!* Then his spirit took over. He felt immediately repentant as the Spirit flashed something Gabby said to him: "I got to make a few phone calls tomorrow to apologize . . . " Of all the powerful, emotional, spirit-shaking things God had revealed to Solomon through Gabby, that was the one he would have voted least likely to matter. Yet, it was precisely what God wanted him to do. He couldn't go back in time and undo his mistakes, but it was time to reconcile—to make amends.

Fear suddenly gripped him as he stood up. *How is Errol going to react?* But he knew this must be the first step in his new walk with God, a walk that meant trusting Him, regardless of the outcome. So he girded himself up and jogged over to the couple.

"Excuse me," he shouted. Solomon had a moustache and beard the night he assaulted Errol, so the young man didn't immediately recognize his attacker as he approached. "Errol, I owe you an apology."

Errol was taken aback. "How do you know my name?"

"I am Solomon Trudeau. Last month I assaulted you. I am truly sorry. I never should have touched you, and I know I deserve whatever punishment the courts dish out, but I just wanted to tell you that I know how wrong I was. Can you find it in your heart to forgive me?"

Errol was shocked as he started to recognize Solomon. But that shock almost immediately morphed into a vengeful rage. He pulled his arm from around his date and lunged at Solomon. He punched Solomon twice, knocking him to the ground, all the while cursing at the middle-aged man.

"Errol, stop!", his date screamed. But Errol was having none of that. He had been aching for the chance to find that S.O.B. who sucker punched him in front of everyone. His only regret was no one could see him whoop his tail. He pushed his date away so hard she flew backward a couple of feet and slammed her backside onto the sidewalk. Errol wheeled back around to continue his attack, but the momentary pause she had created allowed Solomon to get his bearings. As the young man attacked, Solomon channeled his training from years past. He blocked the incoming blow and used the boy's momentum to flip him over onto the grass.

"Errol, please! I don't want to fight you. I am truly sorry. Please stop!" Errol jumped back up, not just angry, but embarrassed. He came at Solomon with a hard right cross that Solomon easily avoided. Then Errol countered with a flailing left that Solomon caught and twisted, sending Errol to the ground. Solomon held Errol's arm in the twisted position to keep the boy on the ground and stop the attack. "Young man! Please, I am not your enemy. I don't want to hurt you, and I don't want to ruin your date. Please calm down. The same anger you feel now is the same anger that caused me to hit you for no good reason. Don't let it consume you! Please."

The pain in Errol's contorted arm and Solomon's measured words helped him to calm down. "Alright, alright! We're good."

Solomon released his grip and helped the young man up. "Errol, you should go help your friend up now." Errol didn't seem too bothered by the fact that his date lay there on the ground, stunned and bruised by his hand. He walked over, reached his hand down and said flatly, "Come on, let's go."

The young lady was not so quick to move on, though. She was shocked at how easily her handsome beau morphed into a rage-filled ruffian. "I'll be fine, Errol. Go enjoy your movie." The young man glared. Affection had dissolved into contempt. It appeared Solomon's initial instinct was right, and now this young lady wrapped in his arms was able to see who lurked beneath. As Errol stalked off toward the theater, Solomon walked over to help the young lady up.

"What was that all about?"

Solomon looked at her and said, "Errol and I had a run-in a while back, and I was in the wrong. I came to apologize. But this was all for you. To help you see what you may have missed. Please, be careful. Wolves can disguise themselves very easily. Do you know the Lord?"

"Yes, sir, I do."

"Good. Please, please, ask Him if the next guy is someone He wants you to be with. Then make sure Holy Spirit is the one guiding the relationship."

"Thank you. I will."

Trusting God didn't yield the outcome Solomon expected or wanted, but it was a greater outcome than he could have imagined. It may not be in Errol's heart to forgive, and God knew it, but if he hadn't gone over there to ask, then that young lady may not have gotten to see who he was underneath until it was too late. *Thank you, Lord. I trust you.*

When Solomon came through the door of his house, Grammy greeted him from the sofa, "Hey, Honey."

"Hey, Mama." Solomon walked over to give her a big hug. "Thank you for your guidance and love this morning. I didn't tell you that, but you helped me, maybe more than you know. The Lord spoke to my heart through you. Thank you."

"You're welcome, Honey, but what happened to you? You've been fighting."

"Not exactly. More like defending myself, but I'm alright. I'll explain it all later. We need to have a family meeting. There are some things I need to share with everyone. Can you make a nice sit-down dinner for four?"

"Four?" Grammy asked. "Who else is coming?"

"I'm inviting a guest."

Grammy smiled. "Of course, Son. Is there something you want me to make?"

"Whatever you decide to cook up is fine by me. Could you do one more thing, though?"

"OK."

"Please call Bethany and ask her to join us over the phone. I need my whole family together for this."

"Will do, Honey."

Solomon kissed his mother on the cheek and then went to The Lord's Room and shut the door.

19

"The thief does not come except to steal, and to kill, and to destroy. I have come that they may have life, and that they may have it more abundantly."

John 10:10

When Simone came home, she found Grammy in the kitchen and the table set for four.

"Hey, Grammy."

"Hi, Baby. How was school and practice?"

"It was cool. Nothing new. What's going on? Who's coming for dinner?"

"Your father has invited a guest."

Simone couldn't help but smile. *Gabby is coming!* "I'll help you. Just let me go put my bag upstairs. Is Daddy home?"

"Yes. He's with the Lord right now."

When Simone returned, she got busy helping Grammy in any way she could. *Tonight's gonna be awesome!* She couldn't wait to ask all the questions that had been piling up since she discovered who the woman was that had captured her daddy's attention. *Where are you from? How did you meet? Do you have any kids? Have you been married before? Do you love my dad?* On and on and on, questions flooded her young, anxious mind.

Solomon had not emerged from The Lord's Room though the sun was nearly set and the food was almost ready. Grammy, and her young assistant, had whipped up a nice menu of short ribs, mashed potatoes, green beans and corn bread. Just as Grammy opened the oven to remove the corn bread, Simone heard a knock at the door.

"She's here!" Simone ran toward The Lord's Room, knocked on the door and said, "Daddy, Gabby's here." Then she ran to open the front door.

"Ms. Sherrie?!" Simone was as disappointed as she was surprised.

"Wow, is that how you greet all your guests?" Sherrie replied, feigning offense.

Simone snapped out of it, realizing how rude she had been to her dear friend and mentor. "I'm so sorry, Ms. Sherrie. Please come in." Simone reached out to hug her and then welcomed her in. "I didn't know you were coming over."

"I can tell. Your father called me this afternoon and invited me over for dinner. My son is having a sleepover at his best friend's house tonight, so it worked out nicely. Your father didn't tell you I was coming?"

"I haven't seen or talked to him since I got home. He's been in his prayer room with the door shut this whole time. We don't bother him when the door's shut unless we absolutely have to. I let him know you were here."

Right on cue, Solomon opened the door. The bruises from his afternoon fracas were still quite evident, but his countenance didn't match. He seemed so serene, as if the past few hours were spent in the world's greatest day spa. And there was something in his eyes the girls hadn't seen in a long time. There was surety. There was purpose. Solomon looked like a man who had zero doubt in what his next steps should be.

"Hey, Honey," Solomon greeted Simone and hugged her tight. Then he turned to Sherrie. "Good evening, Sherrie. Thank you so much for accepting my invitation tonight."

Sherrie responded, "Hello, Pastor. I appreciate the invitation. How could I refuse such a gracious and intriguing request?"

"Intriguing?" Simone asked, instantly brimming with curiosity. "How so? What did you say, Daddy?"

Solomon smiled and said, "Just that there were some things I want to tell all of you tonight."

"Dinner's ready," Grammy interrupted. "Simone, please help me put the food on the table."

Solomon led Sherrie to the dining room table, while Simone skipped off to the kitchen. When she returned to place the food on the table, Solomon turned to Grammy and asked, "Would you mind getting Bethany on the phone?" Grammy nodded and dialed Bethany's number. Bethany answered almost immediately, since she was waiting for the call. Earlier, as requested, Grammy had called her to let her know her father wanted to have a family meeting that night to discuss something very important, and he was inviting a special mystery guest. So she, too, was ultra-curious to know what Daddy wanted to say—and who the mysterious guest was. Now, with the whole family present and the table set, Solomon started the dinner with grace.

"Thank You, Lord, for this precious gift—family. You have

blessed us mightily. You have covered us through the heaviest storms. And You have nurtured us to grow in You and for each other. I thank You for Sherrie, an angel You sent to not only help us through a difficult season, but to be an integral part of this family. Lord, by the power of the Holy Spirit who lives in me, I bless this meal and declare it clean from anything that might be harmful to us. Please, Father, bless this time of family and fellowship. In Jesus' name, Amen."

Solomon opened his eyes and surveyed all the loveliness before him. "Thank you, ladies, for being here, especially you, Sherrie. I know this invitation came out of the blue, and you have your life, so I really appreciate you for being here. It's a shame you couldn't bring Trevor. We'll have to do this again so we can all meet your little man."

"You're welcome, Pastor, and thank you."

"And Bethany, thank you for being here. I know you probably have a hundred other things you could be doing on a Friday evening in L.A., so thanks for taking the time as well."

"Of course, Daddy," Bethany answered over the speakerphone.

"I have some important things I need to share with all of you. First, Sherrie, I want to thank you from the bottom of my heart. You have been a tremendous blessing to Simone and this family. At a very dark moment in her young life, you lifted her up, comforted her and helped her find her strength. God used you in a very special way. And it's a cryin' shame that it took me this long to acknowledge you and thank you properly. You are heaven-sent. God grafted you into this family, and if I had had my head and heart in the right place, I would have seen that long ago. From the bottom of my heart, thank you for being what my daughter needed most, when she needed it the most. You are family, and you always will be."

Sherrie was completely surprised. She expected an apology and explanation for the previous night, but, instead, she received a heartfelt declaration of her place in the Trudeau family. "I . . .

I . . . ," she stammered, trying to process her own emotions. "I don't know what to say. You're welcome. You just bathed my heart in love, and I am speechless. Thank you, Solomon." That was the first time Sherrie had ever called him by his first name. It was a moment that seemed so simple, yet it meant the world to her, because it was the first time she truly felt loved and appreciated by him.

"It was long overdue, Sherrie," Solomon answered. "Simone. I treasure you and Bethany so much. And I am so ashamed of myself for not covering you like I should have."

"Daddy," Simone interrupted, quick to protect her daddy, even if it was from himself. "There's no way you could have known Coach Stevenson was gonna do that! You have always covered me and protected me."

"But, no, I haven't Simone. After the attack, I was here, but I wasn't present. I was a provider, but I wasn't a covering. You needed me to hear you; you needed me to comfort you; you needed me to pray with you and intercede for you, and I didn't do it. I was so absent that God had to send his angel here to save the day." Sherrie smiled sheepishly.

"The enemy comes only to steal and kill and destroy. For a while there, I let him succeed, but not anymore, and never again. Years ago, I made a terrible mistake. I killed someone in Iraq during the war. He was in my unit, and I shot him by accident in the middle of a battle. He died right there in front of me. It tore me apart for a long time. I begged God to save his life, but it wasn't meant to be. I went through a lot of therapy to try and get past the guilt and pain. And I did succeed. I got past it, but I didn't overcome it. This morning, thanks to Grammy, the Lord opened my eyes to the baggage that I have been carrying, baggage that had chipped away at my peace, chipped away at my joy. I let guilt become a part of who I was and all I did. That guilt stopped me from fully trusting God. When your mother passed, it made me trust God even less. And after Simone was attacked, I stopped trusting Him altogether. When you fall that far, it's hard to see your way out of it—or be who your family needs you to be. I've been wallowing in the mud for the past year, but that ends today."

Solomon's were the only dry eyes left. Grammy held her son's hand tightly with one hand and wiped tears away with the other. Bethany sniffled on the other end of the line. Simone rested her chin on clasped hands, letting the tears flow freely. And Sherrie looked at Solomon through watery eyes, wanting to reach over the table and give him a big hug.

Solomon continued: "The revelation God gave me this morning actually began last night, during the conversation I had with Gabby as I drove her home. Thank you again, Sherrie, for making it possible. Through Gabby, the Holy Spirit told me I was bound in chains that had been forged a long time ago. I hope those are tears of joy, because I am free, and I will never walk in bondage again. There are so many people I have wronged as I wasted time in my pit. The most important ones are in this room. That's why I asked you all to be here. I am so sorry for checking out on you this past year."

"I love you, Daddy." Bethany initiated a chorus of "I love yous" from the Trudeau women. Then Simone reached over, took his hand and said, "We forgive you."

Solomon smiled at them all and continued: "The Lord has shown me that this is the beginning of a new season, a season of restoration. It began when I repented this afternoon. I was at the park. I didn't know exactly what He wanted me to do next, but then he made it clear. I saw Errol walking in the park, and I felt God telling me to make amends. So, I walked over to him and apologized for hitting him."

Simone interrupted with a gasp., "Is that what happened to your face? Did he beat you up?"

Solomon smiled. Simone, the youngest one of the bunch, was always the most protective. "He got a couple of good licks in, but nothing I didn't deserve. We didn't have a fight, though. I was able to calm him down before things got out of hand."

"Did he forgive you?" Bethany asked.

"I don't think so, but I prayed for him on the way home." Solomon pointed to his heart and said, "There's some stuff in here eating him up. I don't know what it is, but God will reveal it to him in due time."

"How do you know?" Bethany asked.

"Because I asked Him to," Solomon answered matter-of-factly. "But it's not weighing me down anymore. I made a terrible mistake, and I understand why I made that mistake. If he finds it in his heart to forgive me someday, praise God. But even if he doesn't, I am already forgiven."

The women at the table smiled and nodded, understanding exactly what Solomon meant. "Solomon," Sherrie began. "It's not easy for anyone to be so vulnerable, and for a man to do it in front of his family? I wanted to say this in front of your girls. It takes a very strong man—a real man—to humble himself before your whole family the way you did tonight."

As Solomon looked across the table at Sherrie, something unexpected happened. In that moment, Sherrie seemed to transform. All of a sudden, her hair seemed to almost glow. Her eyes suddenly became a stunning shade of hazel and brown. Her skin morphed into this smooth, soft satin. Even her voice found a new, harmonious pitch that delighted his soul. In that moment, it was as if scales fell from Solomon's eyes so he could finally see just how beautiful Sherrie was. Looking into her eyes, Solomon replied, "Thank you, Sherrie. There's always something beautiful on the other side of a contrite heart and a right spirit."

Recognizing Solomon's subtle flirtation would surely elicit a response from the girls that could spoil the moment, Grammy interjected, "So, what next, Honey?"

"Well, Mama, I gotta take a trip. There's someone I need to see."

"Who is that, Honey?"

"Tim Stevenson."

There was a palpable change in the atmosphere. Simone and Sherrie looked at each other in disbelief. Then Simone declared, "Daddy, you do not need to apologize to him!"

"Oh no, Honey, I'm not going to apologize. I need to forgive him, and I need him to know that. I need to look into his eyes and let him know I forgive him."

"Why not just write a letter?" Bethany asked. "They get mail in prison."

"It's part of my journey, Honey. The Lord wants me to go there and tell him in person."

"Why?" Simone asked.

"Honestly, I don't know. But I know I'm gonna start trusting God, regardless of the outcome. If I trust God, then I don't need to know why. He will reveal it to me in His time, if I just obey and trust Him."

"Do you want us to come with you?" Grammy asked.

"No, Mama, I got this."

"Good," Simone blurted out. "Just 'cause I forgave him doesn't mean I need to see him again—ever."

20

The Lord God said, "It is not good for the man to be alone. I will make a helper suitable for him."

Genesis 1:18

A couple of days after the family meeting, Solomon called the Edenwood State Penitentiary to schedule a visit with Tim Stevenson that weekend. Solomon was very anxious about the meeting. There was still a boatload of animosity toward the man that attacked his daughter. And if it were up to Solomon, there always would be. But this wasn't up to him. The Spirit's leading was clear, and Solomon couldn't let his flesh get in the way. Not again. The rumble in the park opened his eyes to what a lifetime of truly trusting God could be. Rather than stress over the unknowns, he was now relishing the opportunity to play his part in unfolding God's big plan. He hadn't known what God had in store for him as he walked over to Errol that day, but if a minor beat-down at the park could save a young lady from possibly making a terrible mistake, what could He have in mind for this meeting with that pedophile?

The last few weeks had ushered in a spiritual revival within Solomon. His relationship with God grew stronger and stronger with each passing day. It was like a father holding his son in a never-ending embrace because he hadn't seen him in years. It was a new day! No more worrying about how terribly wrong his efforts might turn out. No more worrying about whether he had been a good enough husband to Gloria. No more worrying! Trusting God meant He could let the worries float off into space and just live and love each day. Not knowing what happens next—and not worrying about not knowing what happens next—turned each day into a new adventure, a quest to find out how God would use him over the next twenty-four hours. His daddy once said, "I hope you learn how to take your hands off the wheel and let Him do the drivin', 'cause wherever you're goin' ain't nearly as fun as where He'll take you." Well, it took four decades and some change, plus a whole lot of trials, but Solomon could finally tell his daddy, *I got it, Pop! I got it.*

As God would have it, Solomon wouldn't be making the drive to the big house by himself. After the family dinner, he and Sherrie exchanged quite a few messages. They were cordial, even playful interchanges, but there was a hidden agenda. Since the family meeting, Sherrie felt a desire to see Tim Stevenson as well. She had forgiven him ages ago, but the last time he saw her, she was bottoming out—no scholarship, no track career, no future. She wanted him to know that wasn't the end of things for her. She wanted him to know that, despite all she had done and all she had been through, she was still standing. So, after a couple of days of texting, she worked up the nerve to ask if she could join Solomon on his trip. Solomon definitely didn't mind the company, and, to be honest, he was looking forward to *her* company.

Saturday arrived with a bang, literally. A thunderstorm had rolled in early that morning. Raindrops pounded the roof, and dark clouds made the morning seem to drag on forever. There's no way Solomon was going on a road trip in this weather. *That place has visiting hours all the time; no need to be out in this.* He sat down on the recliner, grabbed the remote and resigned himself to stay home. Just as he tuned in to the college bowl game, the pounding subsided, and the light of day appeared. Solomon sat there for a moment, frozen. His spirit knew what needed to happen, but his body was now Velcroed to the chair, and his mind had already surrendered to the circumstances. *The guy's a convict; he's not going anywhere.* Solomon picked up his cell phone to text Sherrie about the change in plans, but before he could finish the text, his attention was pulled back to the television by the crowd roaring its approval as the opening kickoff was returned for a touchdown. The announcer declared, "If he had hesitated just a second before making that cut, we'd be talking about how he got clobbered, not how he took it all the way!" *Ugh. I hear you loud and clear, Lord.* Solomon texted, "I'm on my way," to Sherrie. He turned the TV off, said goodbye to Grammy and Simone and walked out to his car. He picked up Sherrie, and the two were off to prison.

"Good afternoon, Sherrie."

"Good afternoon, Solomon. Pretty ugly start to the day, right?"

"You're telling me. I was two seconds from calling you to cancel, but I had a pretty clear order not to."

"Really? The Lord's not playin' around."

"Nope. Gotta go, and I gotta go today, evidently. How has your week been?"

"It's been good. Trevor came home from school so excited on Thursday. During PE, they had all the boys race on the track. Guess who was the fastest?" Sherrie smiled with pride, knowing the apple didn't fall too far from the tree.

"Nice. So we got a couple track stars. Maybe he can come watch Simone's meets?"

"That's a great idea! I don't know why I hadn't thought of it before."

"So when do I get to meet Trevor?" Solomon asked.

The question sparked a hint of excitement in Sherrie and sent her radar on alert at the same time. It had been a while since a man expressed a genuine interest in her son, and for it to be a man of Solomon's character and spirit made her want to savor the feeling. But a lifetime of hurt and poor choices made Sherrie supremely protective. Trevor was not just a gift from God, he was entrusted to her by Him. She had to do her best to keep his world safe, even if it meant being lonely in her world.

"Well . . . uh . . . " Sherrie stammered, but the sound Solomon's cell phone playing "Lean on Me" by Bill Withers, interrupted— and saved—her.

"Excuse me," Solomon said. "Let me see who this is. Hello?"

"Hey there, Brother. It's Ken."

"Ken! Good to hear from you. How you doin', my friend?"

"I'm good, Rev. Really good. Some pretty amazing stuff happened that night you prayed for me. I've been itchin' to tell you about it."

"Well, I can't wait to hear, but I got you on speakerphone and Sherrie's sitting next to me. Don't know if you know Sherrie, but she knows you. She's one of the prayer warriors from the mission. Did you want to do this another time when I'm alone?"

"Nope. I've been holding on to this for a minute now. Nice to meet you, Sherrie. I think you're gonna want to hear this as well."

"Hello, Ken. I'm all ears."

"Don't know how much you know about that night, Sherrie, so I'll rewind a little bit. While I was eatin', Rev walked by lookin' all depressed and stuff. He was a new face at the mission, and I could tell he needed a friend, so I took pity on him and let him sit with me." Ken and Solomon both let out one of those ear-rattling guffaws. "Just bustin' your ba- . . . uh, just pullin' your chain, Rev."

"Didn't know I would end up sitting in the boys locker room," Sherrie shot back, with a smile and wink.

"Yeah, I found the Lord, but I'm still looking for my manners, Sherrie. Sorry about that."

"Got you!" Sherrie replied. "Don't think we didn't bust some balls in the girls locker room too."

Ken laughed loudly again. "I knew I liked you for a reason, Sherrie. OK, for real. Solomon prayed for me that night at the mission, and I asked God to set me free. That was great, but what happened next is why I'm calling. Solomon, do you remember Gabby came over to me after you prayed?"

"Yeah, longest hug ever!" Solomon joked.

Ken laughed. "Yeah, but I couldn't let go. I've hugged plenty a' girls in my life, but I have never felt what I felt that night. Holding her was like plugging into an electric heater, but instead of the heat radiating out, it was sinking in. I'm telling you, my bones even got warmer. It felt so good, so powerful, I didn't want to let go, 'cause I didn't want the feeling to end. But it didn't! I still felt it as we walked away. I felt it in the back room. It didn't go away until the next morning."

"My Lord, that is a story!" Sherrie interrupted. "Kinda takes my breath away, Ken."

"Well, open the window, 'cause it gets better. That night, I slept in the alley behind the mission. Well, I tried to sleep. Sherrie, this next part might gross you out a bit. I barely got any sleep that whole night 'cause my body started to mess up real bad. My head started pounding. My heart was pumpin' a mile a minute. I was sweating enough to water the bush I was lyin' next to. My stomach felt like it turned inside out. If I wasn't pukin', I was sh- . . . uh, I was havin' diarrhea. My body hurt from my head to my toes. I started prayin' to God 'cause I thought I was dying. After a few hours of agony, everything started to fade away. And I fell into the deepest, most relaxing sleep I've had in ages. When I woke up, the pain wasn't the only thing that was gone. The itch was gone. That constant hunger for a fix—totally gone! And it's stayed gone. I haven't jonesed for some 'candy' since then."

"What!?" Sherrie blurted out. "Oh my God, that's a miracle! The Lord set you free—overnight! I don't know what else to say but hallelujah!"

Solomon sat strangely quiet. The corners of his mouth were turned up, but he wasn't smiling. The hair on his arms were visibly standing, and his eyes looked as if they were looking past the miles of freeway and vehicles in front. "Ken, there are times when even a pastor is at a loss for words. I am so happy for you and grateful to God for breaking the chains. It's just so overwhelming, I can barely speak. The Lord has just been really showing himself mighty in love lately. Not that He doesn't all the time, but, lately, it's been so powerful, so tangible. It's just beyond anything my mind can grasp. But my heart and my soul are doing cartwheels right now for what he has done for you."

"Amen to that, Brother. Cartwheels are nothing; I've done a few back-flips since that day. I'm seven days clean, which is the longest I've been clean in I don't know how long. I'm in the program at the mission to get my life back together. They put me in detox to make sure I'm for real done with that, and this is the first day I am allowed to call out. I just wanted to say thank you, Solomon. I wish I had better words to say, but I'm not a poet. I love you, brother. You saved my life."

"Ken, you've spoken more powerfully and affected me more deeply than any poet could. I'm just so blessed to be a part of your journey. Understand something, though. To whom much is given, much is required. Have you heard that?"

"Yes, sir, I have. And I will not take my freedom and run. This is the first time I have shared my story, but it won't be the last, not by a long shot. I know He's got something for me to do. Don't know what that is, but whatever it is, I'm all in!"

"So am I, Ken. I can't just open the cell and say, 'You're free. Good luck out there.' You won't be walking this road alone. I know you can't get calls, but you have my number. Whenever you get a phone pass, give me a shout. And just so you know, the Lord already started working through you that same night. What you said to me ministered to me—deeply. In fact, I'm on my way right now to deal with some baggage I've been carrying around for a while. I didn't bring it back from the desert, but it's a direct result of what I did bring back. So, your word to me and your prayer is setting me free as well."

"Well, I'll be dam- . . . uh, well, that's f-in' awesome, Solomon. Gotta admit, I have no clue what I said, but happy to know it helped."

"It did. *You* did."

"Well, my ten minutes are up. I'll holler at ya next weekend. Nice meeting you, Sherrie."

"It was an absolute pleasure, Ken," Sherrie replied. "God bless you, and I'll be praying for you."

"Be strong, Brother. I'll talk to you later."

After about fifty minutes of driving, Solomon and Sherrie could finally see the prison in the distance. Such a bleak and morbid place! Prison ministry was never something Solomon felt called to do, and he was grateful for it. Something about the place sent shivers down his spine. Maybe it was the desolate landscape that seemed to echo the desolate souls behind the walls. And those walls! Towering mounds of faceless stone topped by enough razor wire to shred a human being to pieces. And so massive with so few windows, as if they were made to force every wayward soul inside to choose between looking up to God or looking out at the misery of captivity. Solomon's one night in jail was the closest he had ever come to prison, and it was closer than he had ever wanted to be to prison—until today.

As Solomon pulled into the surprisingly small parking lot, the enormity of the task ahead became more and more oppressive. *I'm about to be face-to-face with the man who attacked my daughter. I have to forgive someone I would happily beat to a pulp.* He tried to present the strong minister's face that he thought he should, and then he realized just how contrary that was to his new walk. *Why put up a false face? Why pretend to have it all under control? How does trusting God square with being too prideful to be honest with Him?* Pretending he's got it all under control would be just putting up another façade, and he knew why he would be doing it—Sherrie. Deep down he didn't want Sherrie to see him as less than the strong, confident, Holy Ghost-filled pastor he hoped she saw him as. *Don't go backward, Solly. Trust God.*

Solomon parked the car and slowly reached forward to turn the engine off. Sherrie could sense the sudden shift in his aura. This meeting wasn't nearly as impactful to Sherrie. Though Tim Stevenson took advantage of his position, and her youthful naiveté and inner turmoil, she knew it was neither coerced nor her first. So, the wound was neither deep nor fresh. She looked at Solomon and asked, "Is everything ok?"

"Sherrie, I . . . I need to be honest with you, and with myself, and with God. I'm terrified right now. I don't like prisons; I really don't like prisons. And I don't know if I can forgive this man. It seemed so clear and easy the other day. Heck, it seemed so easy fifteen minutes ago! But now, I just . . . I . . . will you please pray for me?"

This strong, handsome man of God was being not only transparent with her, but vulnerable. And in his vulnerability, Sherrie saw more strength than she had ever experienced with any man. She looked deeply into his eyes and saw a soul yearning to be free yet wrestling with the very real—and righteous—anger that still burns. It had been a long time since a man needed her the way Solomon needed her right now. And until that very moment, she didn't realize how good it felt, and how much she missed being needed like that. Then it became clear: *I'm not here to tell*

Coach Stevenson 'I made it'; I'm here for Solomon!

So, she turned toward Solomon, and with a look of pure love in her eyes, extended her hands toward him. Sometimes a well-placed word can relieve pain and lighten a heavy burden, but her silence, her strength and the steadfast love in her eyes spoke louder than a sonnet and was as clear as a still, soft voice. Solomon grabbed her hands and lowered his head.

"Father God, blessed by your precious name. This truly is the day that you have made, so we rejoice to be in it. I lift up Solomon to you, Lord. Your word tells us to anger, but not sin. You know Solomon has every right to be angry, and we know that You share his anger. The tears he's cried, You cried. But You didn't call us to bondage, but to freedom. Please, walk with Solomon today. Let him feel You at each step, --Your perfect peace, Your divine presence. Let Your Spirit reign in him. Let Your Spirit strengthen him. Let Your Spirit lead him to freedom from the shackles of unforgiveness, because whom the Son sets free is truly free indeed. We can endure all things, Lord, through You, who gives us strength. And by Your stripes, Lord, we are healed. So, let Your healing fall on Solomon and Coach Stevenson today so that You may be glorified in another soul repaired and renewed. In Jesus' name, Amen."

"Thank you, Sherrie. I'm ready."

21

"And we know that in all things God works for the good of those who love him, who have been called according to his purpose. For those God foreknew he also predestined to be conformed to the image of his Son, that he might be the firstborn among many brothers and sisters."

Romans 8:28-29

The ominous appearance of the prison assaulted one's eyes, but the destitute, sinister atmosphere in the prison assaulted one's spirit. Every gate that closed felt like another step down to the abyss. The guards were neither amiable nor helpful, appearing every bit as trapped as the men they secured. The walls were painted in a drab light gray hue that was clearly intended to neither excite nor incite all those unfortunate enough to be immersed in it. Prison was everything Solomon thought it would be—and everything he couldn't wait to get away from.

The guards ushered Solomon, Sherrie and a host of other visitors into a large, open room with cafeteria tables and benches. Only the most hardened criminals are kept separated from their guests by plexiglass, and it would seem the prison system didn't put Tim Stevenson in that category. This only exacerbated Solomon's anxiety over his impending meeting.

"I hope they don't think we're family," Solomon said with an uneasy laugh. But he was anything but jovial. The last time he saw this man, Solomon attacked him like a supremely pissed-off dad. Now he had to sit, with no barrier, a couple of feet across from the man who attacked his little girl—with the smoldering fires of old anger stoking fresh embers by the second—and forgive him. Sherrie sensed the tug-of-war between Solomon's spirit and his flesh. Without saying a word, she gently held his hand and began to intercede for him in her heart.

A loud bell indicated the prisoners were about to enter the room. Solomon took a deep breath, as if to say, "Here we go." The guards opened a door at the opposite end of the room. Tim Stevenson shuffled in, the sixth prisoner in a line of almost twenty. The bright-orange jumpsuit hung loosely on his lean frame. He looked around to see who had come to visit him. None of his family said they were coming, so this was one of the few, hopefully pleasant, surprises in his dreary, monotonous and frightening reality. When his eyes spied table No. 6, they almost bulged out of their sockets. *Solomon Trudeau!* He was the last person Tim Stevenson expected to see. Standing next to him was his old pupil and paramour, diminutive in stature, but powerful in presence. This was not the pleasant surprise he was hoping for. He walked toward the table a little slower, unsure how guarded he needed to be. *Last time I saw this man, he wanted to kill me. And Sherrie, why would she want to visit me in here? With him?*

"Hello, Mr. Trudeau. Good afternoon, Sherrie. This is quite a surprise."

Solomon stood frozen, silent. His tongue was bonded to the roof of his mouth. Tim Stevenson extended his hand to shake Solomon's. It was greeted with stale air. He turned it to Sherrie. She reached across the table and returned the cordial gesture. They all sat down, and there was silence for a moment, no one really knowing where or how to begin. Finally, the disgraced Olympian broke the silence.

"Mr. Trudeau, sir," he began. His respectful tone was not born of just a repentant heart, but also a cautious one. He could sense Solomon was just one misplaced word away from a full meltdown. "I am truly sorry for what I did to Simone."

"Really?" Solomon fired back, involuntarily rising from his seat. "Is that why you pled not guilty and had the nerve to smile and wink at her sister after her statement!?" The silent prayer, and the gentle touch of Sherrie's hand on his thigh, brought a measure of temperance back to him.

"Wink?"

"You don't remember, eh? I saw it with my own eyes, and I will never forget it. She had just given her statement and sat down when you looked at her and smiled and then winked at my other daughter. It lit a fire in me that's still white-hot right now! Only God, and Sherrie, are keeping me from—" Solomon stopped, feeling his anger perilously close to erupting.

The scene came back to Coach Stevenson. He remembered that day vividly, the day his would-be victim confronted him in court and made him feel like the absolute scum of the earth. "Mr. Trudeau, I remember that day well. That was the day a young girl opened my eyes. Your daughter broke me that day. I couldn't even look at her after she spoke. I was so full of shame because she showed me what I had become. But then I heard my mother whimper. I looked at her and did something to make her feel better, something she and I have shared since grade school. I winked at her. Mr. Trudeau, she was sitting directly in front of your oldest daughter. That wink was to my mom, not her."

Revelation! That day in court was stamped into Solomon's psyche, but all of a sudden the image became clearer, as if his memory had suddenly upgraded to ultra-high definition. He remembered the elderly woman sitting in front him. He remembered that she was the coach's mother. He remembered seeing Tim Stevenson winking at her many times when he entered the courtroom. *Why didn't I see that then?*

"Sherrie, I am so sorry for taking advantage of you," Coach Stevenson continued. "I used my position, and I exploited your vulnerability like a predator with no conscience. Mr. Trudeau, I am sorry for what I did to Simone. I am sorry for what I did to your family, to all the women and families I hurt. I can't fathom the pain my actions caused, and may still be causing. I deserve to be here, and Simone helped me see that.

"I was a sexual predator, and I will carry that terrible shame for the rest of my life. I had grown so full of myself I couldn't even see the man—the mess—I had become. I had become drunk with myself; I was just hubris and testosterone. The day I tried to force myself on Simone, I was a monster, not a man. I had never been violent with any woman, until that day with Simone. To this day, I still don't know what came over me. It's easy to say the devil made me do it, but the truth is, I literally blacked out. I remember stretching Simone, and I remember her stomping my knee and running away. I was so sure of my innocence that I pled not guilty.

I just knew I couldn't have done what I was being accused of. Why would I rape anyone? I was so convinced of my own superiority that I couldn't imagine a woman not wanting me, so why would I take something that is freely given? Even after the verdict, I just knew I was being railroaded.

"But then, Simone spoke. And her words cut through me like a knife through warm butter. It didn't matter if I remembered it, I knew she was telling the truth. I knew I did what she said. At that moment, I realized for the first time, I attempted to rape a little girl." Coach Stevenson began to cry, flooded with remorse and shame. Drawing courage from a well he didn't know he possessed, he lifted his head, looked straight into Solomon's eyes and uttered words no father is prepared to hear, "I tried to rape your little girl."

Tears flowed down Coach Stevenson's cheeks, as well as Sherrie's. Sherrie looked across the table and, for the first time, saw his brokenness. Tim Stevenson wasn't the same man who took advantage of her. Solomon remained stone-faced, unwilling to give the man across from him any reprieve from his morass of guilt. But his poker face belied the transformation under way in his heart. That moment—the smile and the wink—was the trigger that had dropped him into an emotional and spiritual cavern. And now he knew that trigger was a mirage. His daughter's attacker hadn't actually mocked and marginalized her during her moment of triumph. Solomon realized he hadn't been holding on to righteous anger all this time, but vengeful wrath. And with a few honest words from Coach Stevenson, Solomon could look across the table and begin to see a man—a soul—rather than a predator.

"I spent every day after that coming to grips with what I had done," Coach Stevenson went on. "Not just to Simone, but what I did to you, Sherrie, and all the other women—girls. Even now it's still so hard for me to say that. It's a terrible thing to be so in love with yourself that you can't even see innocence, let alone honor it and protect it. You may never forgive me or believe me, but I thank God he brought you here today, because I needed to tell you I'm sorry, and I am not that man anymore. I will never be that man again. Sometimes God has to let you fall to the bottom before you can see yourself for who you really are. I repented and rededicated myself to the Lord since coming here. I refuse to be that man, and I'm feeding my spirit daily, because I know what lurks in this flesh. He's dead and I'm keeping him buried him under six feet of word and prayer."

Solomon could tell Coach Stevenson had said all he had to say. He folded his arms and looked down at the table as if his next words were inscribed in the dull metal. In it he saw the anger he had stored because his baby had been attacked; he saw the wrath he had stored because of a perceived slight; he saw the guilt he had stored because he had left his daughter alone; he saw the shame he had stored because he had let the devil succeed in pulling his hands from the plow. Solomon saw what he had been holding onto, and who he had become as a result. And, then, he heard it. A gentle quiet voice, smooth as a spring meadow and certain as the ground beneath his feet. A voice that at once came from everywhere, and nowhere.

"Let it go."

Solomon looked up to stare directly into the former coach's eyes with a cold, almost malevolent gaze. But then, the edges of his eyes softened; he relaxed his jaw, and he unfolded his arms. The corners of his mouth turned upward just a bit, offering the first hint of peace in him since the prison first appeared on the horizon. After a deep breath, Solomon said, "Tim, I forgive you. Be at peace." With that, Solomon stood up, nodded his head slightly toward the flabbergasted and grateful former coach, turned, and walked toward the door.

22

Then Jesus said to his disciples, "Whoever wants to be my disciple must deny themselves and take up their cross and follow me."

Matthew 16:24

Solomon had driven almost an hour for a meeting that took less than ten minutes, but the catharsis he experienced because of it, and the company of one increasingly enchanting woman, made the ride home feel like a pleasant stroll in the park. As one chapter closed, a new one was being written. Solomon and Sherrie traded stories, knowingly passing the time, but unwittingly intertwining their spirits.

As they got a little closer to Sherrie's home, Solomon realized just how much he enjoyed talking to her. "If you're not sick of my company, would you like to have dinner with me?"

Sherrie looked at the man behind the wheel as if she had suddenly become a shy freshman being asked to the prom by the quarterback of the football team. She was giddy inside, more than happy to let the courtship continue. But the other "man" in her life was more important. She told Trevor she would be back in time to make him dinner, and she always kept her word to him.

"Well, as wonderful as that sounds, I told Trevor and the babysitter I would be home in time to make dinner. But I'll gladly take a rain check, kind sir."

Solomon laughed at the playful formality. "But of course, my lady. You know, you never did answer my question."

"What question?"

"When do I get to meet Trevor?"

"That's right. I didn't. Well, I am very, very cautious about who I bring into Trevor's world. But since you already declared us 'family,' it makes sense you should meet my little miracle, but my home isn't ready for guests just yet."

"I think I can afford another plate. Let's all go to dinner, the three of us."

"It's a date! I'll call my babysitter and ask her to get Trevor ready."

As Sherrie picked up her phone to make the arrangements, Solomon noticed the exit for Trinity Community Church was coming up. He felt almost compelled to take the exit. But he didn't know why. "Sherrie, I have to make a quick pit stop at my church."

"OK. How long before we will pick up Trevor?"

"Maybe fifteen minutes."

Solomon took the exit and parked in the parking lot shortly thereafter. He didn't know why he was there. The church offices were closed. Only the prayer garden was open. Solomon stepped out of the car, still perplexed at why the Holy Spirit led him there. He walked up the steps and checked the doors. As expected, they were locked. He walked around the side of the church to the prayer garden, sat down, and closed his eyes to pray. A gentle touch on the shoulder interrupted him. He turned and saw no one. But something caught his eye on the ground, in the corner of the garden. He got up and walked over. As he brushed aside some leaves, there rested a white clergy collar. Solomon picked it up with both hands as if it were a precious treasure. Then he nodded his head, looked toward heaven, and said, "Yes, Lord."

Create in me a pure heart, O God, and renew a steadfast spirit within me.
Do not cast me from your presence or take your Holy Spirit from me.
Restore to me the joy of your salvation and grant me a willing spirit, to sustain me.

Psalm 51:10-12

Milton Keynes UK
Ingram Content Group UK Ltd.
UKHW022334200923
429086UK00016B/171/J

9 798985 636710